SUDDEN STORMS

Center Point
Large Print

Also by Marcia Lynn McClure and available from Center Point Large Print:

The Bewitching of Amoretta Ipswich
The Secret Bliss of Calliope Ipswich
The Romancing of Evangeline Ipswich
Midnight Masquerade
Shackles of Honor
Divine Deception
The Horseman
Sweet Cherry Ray
The Wolf King
The Pirate Ruse
The Haunting of Autumn Lake

SUDDEN STORMS

MARCIA LYNN McCLURE

CENTER POINT LARGE PRINT
THORNDIKE, MAINE

This Center Point Large Print edition
is published in the year 2025 by arrangement with
Distractions Ink.

Copyright © 2011 by Marcia Lynn McClure.

All rights reserved.

All character names and personalities in this work
of fiction are entirely fictional, created solely in the
imagination of the author. Any resemblance to any
person living or dead is coincidental.

The text of this Large Print edition is unabridged.
In other aspects, this book may vary
from the original edition.
Printed in the United States of America
on permanent paper sourced using
environmentally responsible foresting methods.
Set in 16-point Times New Roman type.

ISBN: 979-8-89164-572-1

The Library of Congress has cataloged this record
under Library of Congress Control Number: 2025932780

To Sheri

For all the glorious adventures we've shared . . .
Photo fun and betta fish sprees,
Belting out ballads in yogurt parlors . . .
And the Sudden Storms of life
we've weathered together.
Thank you for being the blessed and bright
sunshine after the rain . . .
For rare and true friendship to cherish—
and memories like no others in the universe!

Thus, for you . . . some kisses in the rain!

INSPIRATION DEDICATION
To my husband, Kevin . . .
Truly, truly my inspiration in writing!
But also my core inspiration for loving—and
loving life!
I Love You, Kevin from Heaven!

SUDDEN STORMS

CHAPTER ONE

"I'ma comin'. I'ma comin'. Hold your horses," Jolee Gray called. From where she stood at the kitchen window, she couldn't see who was knocking at the front door. Drying her hands on her apron and tucking a loose strand of tawny hair behind her ear, she crossed the parlor to answer it.

"Yes?" she said, as she opened the door and found a young man standing before her. With sudden curiosity, Jolee's fair eyebrows rose above her lovely sky-blue eyes as she studied the boy. He was dreadfully thin, and it was obvious he was uneasy. His oversized hat sat low on his brow, making it nearly impossible for her to see his eyes.

"Hello, ma'am," the boy greeted. Jolee knew at once he must indeed be in his early adolescent years, for his voice was still unaffected by the deepened intonation of a matured man.

"Yes?" Jolee repeated. She smiled at the boy as he nervously twisted the hem of his shirt.

"Um . . . beggin' your pardon, ma'am . . . my name's Tommy Williams, and I was wonderin' if ya might have some chores needin' doin' . . . somethin' that might earn me a meal or two and a place in your barn for a couple of nights," the boy blurted in an uncertain voice entirely lacking in masculinity.

Jolee studied the boy for a moment. "You sure you're up to it, boy? Ya look a might . . ." she began.

"Oh, yes, ma'am! I'm a might small . . . I know. But, I can work like any old horse ya ever seen!" the boy reassured her, nodding adamantly.

Suspicion began to creep to the front of Jolee's mind, and she smiled inwardly as well as out. *This might be a fun little hand to play out,* she thought. She'd go along.

"Well, sure thing! I think I can put ya to work 'round here. At least for a few days. No doubt my brother will have some things needin' doin' as well."

"Oh, thank ya, ma'am! I'm most grateful!" the boy sighed with relief as he reached out and shook Jolee's hand in gratitude.

At the first touch of the boy's hand, Jolee's suspicions were confirmed, and she silently congratulated herself on her keen eye. *Yes,* she thought, *this might prove to be a very interesting few days.*

♦ ♦ ♦ ♦ ♦

"Who in tarnation have ya got cleanin' out the stalls, Jo?"

It was Paxton. Jolee giggled at her brother's predictability.

Smiling she answered, "Just a young man needin' somethin' extra to do."

"Well there ain't nothin' at all to him," Paxton grumbled. "Pitches manure like he ain't never seen a pitchfork and a pile before."

Jolee turned and smiled at her brother as he swaggered through the back door leading to the kitchen. "Now, Pax," she began as he worked the pump, rinsing his face with the water it produced. "He's obviously travelin' all alone. And did ya notice how small he is? Probably ain't had a decent meal in weeks. All he wants is a couple of meals and a bed in the barn for a while. I think we can allow that."

Paxton Gray dried his hands and face on the towel his sister handed to him. "We can't be feedin' every dang drifter that hops off the train in Blue River, Jo. 'Sides . . . somethin' ain't right with that boy."

Jolee quickly glanced at her brother. "What ain't right, Pax?"

"Oh . . . I don't know. He's too darn small to be on his own. What if he up and dies out there in our barn tonight of some grisly disease! Then everyone'll think we're infected, and they'll . . ."

"Oh for pity's sake, Pax!" Jolee interrupted with a relieved sigh followed by an amused giggle. "He ain't got any strange sickness. Let the boy work and have a few nights of restin'. Maybe my cookin' will put some meat back on his bones."

"Well, all I'm gonna say is he's your wounded

bird, Jo. I ain't takin' no responsibility about him. You fatten him up and be his mama . . . but I ain't gonna be bothered with it," Paxton grumbled.

Jolee smiled to herself and said, "All right, Paxton. All right. Now, just eat your lunch and get your own self back to workin'."

She set a plate on the table and watched affectionately as her brother enjoyed the ham and biscuits. Tipping her head to one side, she studied her brother's rugged and absurdly handsome face. His own sable-smooth hair was a bit mussed from the day's required chores, but his eyes were as brilliant a blue as ever. She thought on them a moment, noting how they held the tranquil blue of a robin's egg one instant, and the next caused a person to shiver with trepidation. When Paxton was vexed or provoked, the tranquil sky-blue of his eyes turned stormy, and even Jolee could be unsettled by their intensity.

Jolee stood behind her brother and ran her hands the breadth of his strong shoulders. She wondered then at the true age of the young person outside cleaning Paxton's stalls as she said, "Paxton Gray . . . you're wastin' this fine form Mama and Daddy blessed you with. Tall, fine, handsome men like you shouldn't wait so long to settle down. Ya oughta find ya a cute little girl and . . ."

"Ah," Paxton growled, brushing his sister's hands from his shoulders. "Don't ya go startin' in on me again, Jo. You go ahead and work ol' Weston Warner into your weddin' bed, and then ya can talk to me about such nonsense as marryin'."

Jolee bent and kissed his cheek affectionately. "Me and Weston Warner? What're ya goin' on about? Such silliness I never did hear. Now, eat your lunch and leave that boy I hired alone," she scolded. A knowing smile broke across her face, however. Glancing out the window into the beauty of the day, she nodded. She had a feeling. And Jolee Gray's feelings had never steered her wrong.

◆ ◆ ◆ ◆ ◆

"Well, Tommy," Jolee began as the boy stood waiting her instruction. "Why don't ya carry some water to the tub for my brother's bath tonight? That's somethin' I like to do for him after he's been workin' hard all day. He don't run me, mind you. But he gets so awful sore and tired. I already have the pot on the stove heatin'. You can carry some cold water in buckets from the pump at the sink."

The boy nodded and within a few minutes had a nice, smooth routine going. Fill a bucket from the pump, lug it into Paxton's bedroom where the tub sat, and empty it in.

"It's nearly full, ma'am," the boy announced directly.

"That's fine, Tommy. Pax will be in any minute.

Here." Jolee handed the boy two folded towels and pointed to the pot of boiling water sitting on the stove. "Now, lug that on in, and pour it into the rest. Be careful! We don't want ya burnt, now do we?"

The pot was extremely heavy, and Rivers wasn't at all certain she could carry it to the bedroom. The steam from the boiling water stuck to her face, causing her discomfort.

Setting the pot on the floor in front of the tub at last, Rivers stood up and arched her aching back. She was glad Jolee Gray had let her do some chores around the farm. She did indeed need a good meal and shelter, but she was beginning to tire rapidly now that the day was drawing to a close. Her hands, arms, and legs were sore from the strenuous work, and she hated having to wear a hat! It stifled her so. Especially when she wore it pulled down so far over her brow. Still, she'd found a kind soul in Jolee Gray.

What a kind person Jolee seemed to be. Rivers guessed Jolee must be close to her own age. She was small like Rivers, yet sturdy looking. The woman's blue eyes and golden hair had a serene and calming influence on Rivers's tired and anxious state. It seemed Jolee was a lovely woman within and out.

Rivers thought of her own dark brown hair and black-brown eyes. She'd always felt her features were too severe. Her skin was fair, but her hair, eyes, and eyelashes were varying shades of dark brown. She had never been able to see a trace of beauty in herself. She had almost been able to convince herself once that her mouth was pretty enough. Her perfectly shaped lips held a natural red ripe-cherry color that she found herself having to disguise with dust and chapping when she was riding the trains. But even with that one claim to possible beauty, Rivers had known she was only fooling herself. And considering her circumstance, it was all the better. If she had been some dazzling beauty, Jolee would have known instantly that Rivers was, in fact, a young woman and not an adolescent boy searching for work.

Rivers's mind quickly left Jolee then. That man—Jolee's brother! A heavy sigh of admiration escaped Rivers's lungs at the thought of him. When he'd come upon her in the stall out in the barn, she felt sure he suspected. He'd stood glaring down at her for several moments and then, without a word, turned and determinedly strode away.

He was frightening after a manner. His frown, for one thing—so severe and intense. Still, he was the most physically appealing man Rivers had ever seen in all her life! Tall, broad-shouldered, onyx-black hair, square and unshaven jaw, piercing blue eyes. He was astonishing! The mere sight of him had caused Rivers's heart to miss several beats—caused her to feel breathless and overheated. His physical build was as flawless as his face, and he moved with an incredibly intimidating air of confidence and determination. This Paxton Gray was, from all outward appearances, an embodiment of perfect masculinity.

Rivers had been so greatly relieved when he had left her to her work. And now, she was anxious to leave his bedroom before he arrived for his evening bath.

Lifting the great pot of water, she began pouring it into the tub. Then having finished, she set it down again and said out loud, "There now."

"Thank ya kindly, boy."

Whirling around, Rivers gasped in horror as she saw Jolee's brother standing before her in the process of removing his clothing. He grinned at her in a friendly manner, revealing one long, thin dimple on his left cheek at the corner of his smile. He'd already stripped his shirt from his broad torso; his trousers, too, lay in a heap at his feet. The man was nearly finished unbuttoning his flannels. As he peeled the garment from his arms, Rivers turned to face the other direction.

"Pardon me, sir," she apologized.

"You're a bashful little feller, ain't ya?" the man noted, and Rivers held her breath when she heard him disturb the tub of water as he stepped into it.

"Aaahhh," he sighed. "Ain't nothin' like a warm soak after a long day. Ain't that right, boy?"

"Um . . . yes, sir," Rivers agreed, stepping sideways toward the door.

"Hold up there, would ya? Hand me that there brush and lye 'fore ya run off, young feller," the handsome man commanded.

Rivers saw the brush and soap lying on top of a trunk sitting before her. Swallowing hard, she reached out, taking hold of them. She took several steps backward, keeping her eyes on the wall directly in front of her. Holding the items firmly, one in each hand, she stretched her arms out behind her.

"Thank ya kindly," the man said. An unsettling sensation akin to some sort of delightful shiver wracked her as he took them from her. "You can be on your way now, boy."

Rivers rushed from the room and slammed the door tightly behind her. She could hear the man chuckling. He must think her an odd duck indeed.

"There ya are, Tommy. Come have a plate," Jolee coaxed, motioning toward the kitchen table.

Jolee smiled to herself. The girl was as red as a radish. *Leave it to Paxton,* she thought. No doubt he'd nearly dropped his drawers right there in front of her! Still, if Paxton was too mule-stubborn to see what was standing right before his eyes, then it served him right. She wondered how long the girl's pretending would go on before Paxton figured it all out.

She sighed and shook her head. Knowing her brother as she did, the girl could be doomed to masquerade as a boy forever.

The food Jolee had prepared was pure satisfaction to Rivers. It had been so long since she'd had a decent meal. She enjoyed it thoroughly, savoring every morsel so her mind could think back on it when tougher times came again. She looked up when she'd finished to see Jolee smiling pleasantly at her.

"Ya know, Tommy," Jolee began. "Ya really should take your hat off before sittin' down to a meal."

Rivers dropped her head self-consciously. "Beg your pardon, ma'am."

"Well, ya ought to . . . even when you're just enterin' the house, to be honest," Jolee added.

Rivers did not respond but only continued to eat. Hopefully Jolee would leave the subject be.

"Jo!" came the booming, masculine voice from the other room.

Rivers stiffened in her chair as she heard the door leading from the room where Jolee's brother was bathing open.

"Jolee! There ain't one pair of clean flannels

in my chest-a-drawers! What do ya expect me to do? Catch my death of cold sleepin' in my birthday suit?"

Rivers jumped anxiously in her chair as the man strode in and stopped directly beside her. He stood with only a towel wrapped about his waist and nothing else to cover him.

"For pity's sake, Pax! You're drippin' all over my clean floor! Towel off before ya go trampin' through the house!" Jolee scolded.

The proximity of the unclothed man caused Rivers's reflexes to spring her from her chair so violently that it toppled over backward, crashing to the floor.

"He sure is a jittery little feller, ain't he?" the man said to his sister.

Rivers mumbled an apology and bent to pick up the chair. Her gaze fell spontaneously to Paxton's feet, standing in a small puddle of water rapidly accumulating around them. Rivers couldn't stop her eyebrows from rising in astonishment as her gaze involuntarily continued up the length of his solid, muscular calves. As she stood, replacing the chair, her eyes traveled over his stomach, chest, and arms. His own fabulous eyes were fastened on her when she straightened at last, looking him full in the face.

His hair hung dripping wet about his head, and he said, "You all right there, boy?" Rivers could only nod in response. "Well then, where might a drownin' man find his flannels, Jolee?" he repeated, sighing with impatience at his sister.

Jolee giggled. "I'm sorry, Pax. I plum forgot to bring 'em in off the line. I'll run out and get a pair." With a sideways glance and mischievous smile at Rivers, she left.

Rivers squirmed uncomfortably. Standing in a stranger's kitchen with a scantily clad man was most disconcerting. Even so, she couldn't keep her eyes from straying once more to the magnificently broad shoulders and chest boasted by Paxton Gary. He was perfect! Rivers had seen many men, cowboys, rail-riders—but never had she seen the likes of Paxton Gray.

She jumped as he spoke unexpectedly and slapped her soundly on one shoulder. "Don't worry there, boy. You'll fill out soon enough too. Shoot . . . I was nearly as wormy lookin' as you are when I was your age."

Rivers cleared her throat and cast her gaze down to the floor once more.

He continued, "Tell ya what . . . I reckon it's been a while since ya had yerself a real tub bath. You go on in there . . . the water's still warm enough. Have yerself a good long soak."

Rivers looked up quickly, shaking her head. "Oh, no, no, no. But thank ya all the same."

Paxton Gray frowned. "Now look here, boy . . . Jolee don't go in for smelly men. You had better get yerself in there and bath up."

• • •

Paxton had seen this boy pitching manure earlier in the day and knew he must be in need of a bath. Maybe Jolee liked taking in these motherless pups, but if they were gonna eat under his roof, they were gonna do it cleaned up!

"Now, you go on in there and get yerself washed. I didn't leave the water too all soapy," he repeated, trying to remain calm.

"Um . . . I think I better be gettin' on out to the barn, if ya don't mind, sir," the boy muttered.

"Like hell you are, boy!" And having let his temper get the best of him, Paxton hoisted the boy up over his own shoulder and turned toward the bedroom. He was a weasel of a child! It didn't take any effort at all, only one arm to heft him up. Good thing, too, considering Paxton was tightly holding his towel at his waist with the other hand.

"No! Please!" the boy hollered.

"Now, you soap up. We bath up quite frequent 'round this house," Paxton grunted, dropping the boy bottom first into the tub of water. "And 'cause I know you're unusual bashful . . . I'm gonna leave ya in here . . . trustin', mind you . . . trustin' you'll wash your own self," he warned, pointing a finger at the boy. "I don't wanna have to come back in here and scrub ya down, you hear?"

"Yes, sir," the boy stammered. Paxton fancied

for a moment the child was near to bawling. The boy better toughen up quick or he wouldn't get nowhere in life at all!

"What in tarnation have ya done, Pax?" Jolee scolded as she saw her brother coming out of the bedroom, a triumphant grin on his face.

"That boy needs a good washin', Jo," he stated.

Jolee rolled her eyes and put her hands squarely on her hips. "So ya took it upon yerself to see he done it, is that it?"

Paxton nodded. "Shore 'nough," he confirmed.

Jolee shook her head and threw the flannels she'd gathered at him. "You're too tender-hearted, little sis," Paxton grumbled as he stomped away into the parlor. "A man can't even put on his underwear in his own bedroom 'round here," he muttered as he went. "Gotta be draggin' every stray thing for miles around in here to patch up, don't ya, Jo?"

"And you're as blind as a bull with his eyes poked out, big brother," Jolee retorted. Then going to the closed bedroom door, she said, "There's a towel right there on the chest, Tommy."

"Thank ya, ma'am," came the timid reply.

"I'm goin' on to bed now . . . you go ahead and slip out to the barn when you're finished, all right? I'll leave ya a clean pair of flannels out here, 'cause I know for a fact that Pax didn't take the time to strip ya 'fore he flung ya in there."

"Yes, ma'am."

Jolee Gray shook her head. Paxton—the man couldn't see past the nose on his own face.

CHAPTER TWO

Paxton quietly opened the barn door. He was fairly certain what he suspected was true, and he was pure and simple enraged about it. Jolee was a good woman, and he didn't like the idea of her kindness being taken for granted.

Holding his lantern high and looking around the dark interior of the building, he saw the little weasel. There he was! Sound asleep on a pile of straw over in the northeast corner like there wasn't a thing in the world to worry about.

Paxton was careful where he stepped as he walked to where the boy slept so peacefully. Standing directly above the little beggar, he glared furiously. He hunkered down next to the brat and set the lantern aside.

It was just as he thought. Paxton could tell now, especially with the bulky clothing gone. Beneath a pair of his very own white flannels was the form and figure of a young woman—not an adolescent boy! He shifted the lantern upward a bit, and a frown wrinkled his brow as he examined the purely feminine features of the girl's face. His dunking her in the tub must have washed off the dirt she'd no doubt purposefully applied to her face in order to hide her gender.

Even he, Paxton Gray, was profoundly impressed with what lay there in the straw. He'd never seen eyelashes so thick and long. Her lips were perfectly shaped and crimson as a cherry. Her hair was long and wavy, and he imagined when the eyes were open and no longer shaded by the ugly hat she'd been wearing— well, no doubt her eyes were beautiful in their brilliance, entirely enticing.

Shaking his head to dispel thoughts of admiration, he tried to replace them with the angry ones he'd entertained a moment before. Roughly, he took the girl's chin in one hand.

"Wake up!" he growled. The thickly lashed eyes fluttered open, and a small hand gripped his own, trying to pry it from the lovely face it held. "What're you about, girl?" he demanded. He was astonished then to feel a sharp object pushing against his stomach.

"Let go! Don't you dare to touch me!" the girl cried fiercely.

Suddenly realizing what she must think his intentions were, Paxton chuckled and assured her, "Don't flatter yerself, honey. I just don't go in for liars sleepin' in my barn." He gripped her wrist, squeezing it as hard as he could.

"Ouch!" she cried out, dropping the knife.

"Now, you stand up here," he ordered, pulling her to her feet. The physically dominant man doubled over in the next instant, however, when the girl's knee met his belly with immense force, causing him to lose his hold on her. She darted for the barn door, but Paxton turned, catching her ankle and sending them both tumbling to the barn floor. As she kicked and thrashed, he pulled her toward him until she was fully beneath his heavy, overpowering body.

"You little devil!" he growled as he sat on her legs, catching both of her hands and holding them pinned to the ground above her own head.

"Let me go!" she cried out.

Paxton reached over to where a length of rope lay nearby and pulled it to him, first tying her hands together and then her knees.

"There now. If you're gonna act like an ornery little heifer—I'm gonna treat ya like one," he said.

Pulling her to her feet, he swiftly lifted her and flung her over one broad and very capable shoulder. He walked back to the straw pile and retrieved his lantern. "We'll just see what Jolee has to say about all this now," he muttered as he carried the girl back to the house.

"What's all that racket?" Jolee asked as she rushed into the kitchen in time to see Paxton hauling something into the house. "Paxton Gray! What are ya doin'?" she cried as she realized what it was, or rather who it was, he had slung over his shoulder.

"We got us our own little outlaw here, Jo," he said, striding into the parlor and dumping the girl carelessly onto the sofa.

Jolee looked at the poor young woman. Tears of anger and frustration rolled over her cheeks. Jolee turned to her brother and scolded, "What have ya done? Are ya crazy?"

Paxton looked at Jolee, bewilderment owning his expression as he stated, "It's a girl, Jo."

"I know it's a girl, Paxton. Some of us ain't as blind as you."

"You know? What do ya mean? Ya mean ya knew all along it was a girl?"

"Yes! What have ya done . . . tied her up?" Jolee was horrified. Paxton could be so headstrong and severe. Immediately, she went to the girl and began tugging at the ropes about her knees and wrists.

"If you don't beat all, Jo! What do ya mean lettin' her go on like she was a boy?" he asked angrily.

"Paxton," Jolee began, "I'm sure she has good reason to be dressed up so. I figured she'd tell me when she was good and ready. It sure took you long enough to tumble." Then Jolee looked up at her brother as a curious thought struck her. "When did ya tumble?"

Paxton looked at the girl and frowned. "Ain't never thrown no boy over my shoulder and into a tub that felt like that. Anyway, she looked at me funny when I was standin' next to her in my towel askin' ya for my flannels."

Jolee looked at the girl, face crimson with humiliation and fear. "Well, I can't get these ropes off, Paxton. Dang it all, ya tie 'em too tight," she complained.

Paxton sighed heavily with exasperation and went to where the girl sat on the sofa.

"I only wanted work," the girl explained, staring him straight in the eyes as he fumbled with the ropes binding her.

"Well, why didn't ya tell Jolee that then? She'd a put ya to work in the kitchen or gatherin' eggs," he mumbled.

The girl looked up at Jolee. "I'm truly sorry for deceiving you, Miss Gray. I can only say that . . . that I had my reasons."

Jolee smiled. "Call me Jo. You can't be but a year or two younger than me, can ya?"

The girl winced as Paxton yanked the rope from around her knees. "I'm eighteen, ma'am," she answered.

"Call me Jo. I'm twenty. See? We can be good friends."

"Oh, for cryin' out loud, Jo! She's a drifter! Give her a meal and send her on her way," Paxton said as he wrestled with the ropes still binding the girl's wrists.

Jolee noted the excessive and exaggerated insistence of her brother that she rid them of the girl, and she smiled to herself. "She's gonna stay as long as she likes, Paxton. I need some female company. Especially after listenin' to your borin' chatter day in and day out."

"Thank you, ma'am. But I'll just be on my way now," the girl said as she watched Paxton struggling with his own knots.

"You'll do no such thing! I can use your help 'round here. Besides, you've obviously got nowhere else to get to right away, if ya don't mind my sayin' so," Jolee prodded.

Paxton looked into the girl's face for a moment. She looked quickly away.

"No, ma'am," she said.

"For cryin' out loud! Now we're an orphanage," Paxton muttered as he untwisted the last knotted piece of rope.

Jolee laughed. "He ain't all pickles and vinegar the way he likes to pretend. Now, what's your name?"

"Rivers. Rivers Brighton," the girl replied.

"Well, Rivers Brighton . . . I guess ya got yourself a champeen here in my sister, Jolee," Paxton grumbled.

Jolee watched as her brother straightened his stance and looked down at the girl. Looking to Jolee he said, "I suppose she does get awful tired of my belly achin'." Then he turned back to the girl. "But from here on out you be right upfront with us about everything."

"I'll leave in the mornin'," the girl stated, standing and making to move past him.

Paxton caught her arm. "Hold on there, proud little Patty," he said. "I still got this rope in my hand. If Jo wants ya to stay, she means it. We got an extra room off in the back across from mine. You can stay in there. Maybe I'm a bit old-fashioned, but I don't believe in women toughin' the elements more'n necessary."

"Pax . . . you're as subtle as a thundercloud," Jolee sighed, slapping his hand so he released the girl. "Now, you're gonna stay on here and help me out. I've got green beans and peas comin' up in a week or two, and I can't put 'em all up myself." Jolee took one of the young woman's hands in her own and squeezed it. "You'll stay and keep me company . . . won't ya, Rivers?"

The girl looked quickly at Paxton, who was already sauntering off to go back to bed. "I really don't think I should stay. I just . . ." she began.

"You'll stay," Jolee stated.

Rivers looked back at her and smiled. "I have to earn my keep," she insisted.

Jolee laughed. "Oh, you will! Don't worry about that." Then linking her arm through Rivers's, Jolee led her back to the spare bedroom.

CHAPTER THREE

"It seemed safer that way," Rivers explained, answering Jolee's question.

"You mean from . . . men with . . . bad intentions?" Jolee asked.

"Yes," Rivers admitted softly.

"I'd do the same. Here, beat these eggs for me."

Rivers took the bowl of eggs and began beating them with a fork as she watched Jolee turning the bacon in the skillet.

"Are ya runnin' from somethin', or just travelin'?" Jolee asked.

Rivers liked Jolee even more for her bluntness. She had a "get straight to the point" kind of attitude.

"My daddy was a traveler. I've been riding trains with him for about two years. He passed on a couple of months back," Rivers answered.

"Oh, I'm sorry," Jolee sympathized. "Your mama's dead too, then?"

"Yes. I lived with my mother's parents until two years ago. Then daddy came and took me with him. He said I was old enough to fend for myself if something should happen to him."

"Sounds mighty excitin'!" Jolee lifted the bacon out of the skillet and, taking the bowl from Rivers, poured the eggs into the fresh, hot bacon

31

grease. "Hoppin' trains and all. You must've had some excitin' adventures."

"I suppose," Rivers admitted.

"Well, Jo . . . how's our little bull manure shoveler this mornin'?" Paxton asked as he sauntered into the kitchen, snapping his suspenders into place over his bare torso.

Rivers was feeling a bit more courageous in that moment. Bravely, she turned to face the man. She had no intention of letting him get away with such a mocking remark. "I'm just fine, thank you, Mr. Gray," she remarked. "In fact," she continued as she set a plate piled with griddlecakes on the table and motioned with her head for him to sit down, "I feel like I could put up with just about anyone today." Somehow, knowing they knew the truth about her had renewed Rivers's confidence in her independence during the night.

"Gettin' a little big for our britches this mornin', ain't we?" Paxton muttered as he sat down and began to eat.

Rivers blushed, humiliated with his thinking her ungrateful.

"You ain't forgot the boys are comin' over for cards tonight, have ya, Jo?" he asked his sister.

"No, Paxton. Though I wish I could," Jolee winked at Rivers. "You and I will have to escape to somewhere or another tonight, Rivers. Once a month Paxton and all his smelly men friends get together on a Saturday night and play cards. Now mind you . . . I don't let them gamble anything worth much . . . they use buttons or chore favors or somethin'. But they're plum irritatin', so I usually hide out somewhere."

"My friends don't smell any worse than yours do," the man mumbled.

Rivers couldn't help but admit inwardly that even as grumpy as he seemed to be, he was so handsome it didn't matter. It was difficult not to constantly gawk at him.

Then he addressed Rivers. "You oughta get Jo to lend ya a dress or somethin' to wear 'fore the boys get here. Maybe one of 'em will think you're worth lookin' at, and ya can get yerself married and be taken care of."

Jolee scowled at her brother, handing Rivers the glass of milk she had intended for him.

Rivers took a deep breath. Turning to Paxton she asked, "Do you think so? Do you really think one of them won't care that I'm so helpless and dumb? Do you really think one of them will find me acceptably pretty enough, maybe?"

Paxton looked up at her, his eyes narrowing. "Could be. I wouldn't go bettin' my life on it, but ya never can tell. Some men are taken in easy-like by a young female. Whether or not she's a beauty."

Rivers was furiously hot with anger. She had not a shred of tolerance at his talking down to her. And in the next moment, she simply poured the cup full of milk into his lap.

Slamming the empty cup down on the table in front of him, she shouted, "How dare you? First of all, I'm perfectly capable of taking care of myself! I don't need some smelly old man to do it for me! And second . . . if your friends are as brutal and arrogant as you are . . . what woman on earth with any sense in her head would want one?"

Paxton stood up very slowly. "Jolee," he began calmly, "your little lyin' pail of pig slop just poured milk in my lap."

Rivers was instantly intimidated. He stood so tall and strong before her. The muscles in his arms and chest tensed, overemphasizing each powerful curve. Jolee simply put her hand over her mouth and tried to stifle her laughter.

Paxton glared at Rivers. "You poured milk in my lap," he informed her.

"You . . . you deserved it," she choked out.

Then, in the next moment, as he picked her up and tossed her over one shoulder, she began squealing and beating on his back. Her efforts were useless, however.

"Paxton! Paxton Gray! You put that girl down, do you hear me?" Jolee cried, following as Paxton strode toward the kitchen door.

"My friends ain't old or smelly, girl! And it may be that I am a little rough . . . you're probably

34

one of them girls who like men with lily white skin, smellin' of rose water, and wearin' curls in their hair! Now, in case you ain't never met one, real men smell like sweat! They've got calloused hands and hair that ain't combed out all nice an' purty!" All this he bellowed as he opened the kitchen door, furious as he strode out of the house and toward the creek.

Realizing his intentions, Rivers endeavored to struggle harder. "You put me down this minute!" she cried.

"Real men are too tired to go through all that silly courtin' business! They work from before sun up 'til after it's long gone! Then they fall into bed too worn out to care if they sat out on the front porch swing sparkin' a girl that night or not!"

"Paxton! Don't you do it!" Jolee shouted as she followed him toward the creek.

"I was just tryin' to be nice to ya in there! I don't doubt my friends would take one look at you and swear off women for good! And you go and pour my milk in my lap. Well, I figure it's time ya had another bath!" With that he let her fall bottom first into the creek.

As Rivers sat in the water, the flannel underwear she still wore soaking wet, she looked up at him. She was humiliated, hurt, and angry.

Without further thought of consequences, she reached up, grabbed the waist of his trousers, and, with every ounce of strength in her, yanked

35

him forward. In the next moment, his massive form came crashing down on hers, followed by an enormous splash. He was sitting beside her in the creek.

Rivers stood up, dripping wet, with tears flowing down her cheeks. She tugged at the flannel underwear now clinging wet and heavy to her skin.

"Whether or not I'm pretty and dainty, Mr. Gray . . . I am a woman! And you should treat me as one! Men like you are one reason I began dressing like a boy! If you don't want me here, tell me now! I'll be on my way."

"I don't want ya here," Paxton bellowed, glaring at her from his seat in the creek.

"Fine," Rivers retorted, stomping toward the house.

"Oh, no, Rivers! You have to stay!" Jolee exclaimed.

Rivers turned, completely baffled as the attractive man sitting in the creek began to laugh.

"She's a pistol, Jo . . . I'll say that for her," he said. Then he looked to Rivers. "Ain't a man in this state would dare pull me in the creek, girl! Or dump a cup of milk in my lap, for that matter. I'm sorry if my teasin' offended ya. You can learn to ignore me, can't ya?" he asked. "For Jolee's sake, at least?"

Rivers wiped the tears from her cheeks with the sleeve of her drenched flannels.

"Come on now," he said, extending a hand toward her. "Give me a hand up, and we'll be friends."

Rivers walked back to him. He took her hand as she extended it in an act of truce. But instead of standing to join her, he yanked hard on her arm, causing her to fall forward into the water again. She silently scolded herself for being so utterly gullible.

Paxton stood up chuckling. "Nobody gets the best of me, girl." And he strode away toward the house.

"Ya see, Rivers," Jolee said as they walked back to the house together. "He's not so bad."

"He threw me in the creek!" Rivers exclaimed in dismay.

"Well, just be glad he's taken to ya. It could've been worse."

"Taken to me? You call that taking to me?"

Jolee laughed. "Oh my, yes, Rivers. If you'd been a man, he woulda just broke your nose for dumpin' that milk on him."

♦ ♦ ♦ ♦ ♦

"Don't be scared of her, Paxton," Jolee ventured as she approached her brother in the field later that afternoon.

Paxton hammered fiercely on a nail to hold the barbed wire to the fence post. "What are ya talkin' about, Jo?" he grumbled, though he knew all too well what was coming.

"She's very pretty," Jolee stated.

"That's a matter of opinion."

"You like her," she said, grinning at him.

Paxton took a deep breath and turned to face his sister. He felt sorry for her. She tried so hard for his sake.

"Jolee, let it lie. I ain't fallin' into any more traps . . . ever again. I'm fine as I am. I don't need you tryin' to . . ." he began.

"But she's different, Paxton. I can see you fightin' it," Jolee interrupted.

Paxton chuckled and began hammering once more as he shook his head. "I ain't fightin' nothin', Jo. 'Cept maybe gettin' milk poured in my lap again."

"Oh, you're as stubborn as an old mule, Paxton Gray. You're usin' Ruby as an excuse, and ya know it," Jolee grumbled.

"Ruby ain't got nothin' to do with this. That girl in there is trouble, Jo," he said, raising the hammer and pointing it in the direction of the house. "Trouble, and then some. I can see it."

"Yes. I'm sure ya can, brother." Jolee smiled and turned away. "I'll just bide my time. We'll see, won't we?"

When she'd gone, Paxton stopped his hammering again. He rested his arms on the fence post and looked out across the field.

"Ruby," he said as his eyes narrowed in

remembering. He'd sworn to himself she would be the only woman ever to cause him grief. He'd known for several years no one could ever convince him to trust a woman again—with the exception of his sister. He had sincerely thought for a time that he loved Ruby. The consequences of having been wrong were massive, and now he felt a sort of fear rising within him.

This girl—this beautiful brown-eyed girl who had come into their lives. He'd had an instantaneous attraction to her when he'd seen her lying asleep in the barn. What man wouldn't have? But it was so much more than that. He actually liked her. Or at least he liked something about her. He liked the way she'd poured that milk in his lap. He liked the way she'd looked at him just before she pulled him into the creek.

Nope. Not her. She was trouble and more. Determinedly shaking his head, he resumed the hammering.

◆ ◆ ◆ ◆ ◆

"Let's go out on the front porch for awhile, Rivers," Jolee suggested as the men sat down at the kitchen table for a game of cards.

Rivers was more than happy to oblige. She had felt so uncomfortable meeting Paxton and Jolee's friends. They all looked so bewildered when she was introduced, and she knew there was no doubt they would question Paxton about her being there. Furthermore, she knew he would tell them the entire story—how she had shown up on their doorstep dressed up like a boy—how he had thrown her in the tub, found her in the barn and tied her up, carried her in the house, and so forth.

"Ya look so pretty in my dress!" Jolee exclaimed as the porch swing began to rock to and fro. "I don't think I ever want to wear it again. You just look so perfect in it."

"You are very sweet, Jolee—very skilled with flattery," Rivers recognized, smiling and smoothing the pink and white gingham over her lap. "But I do thank you for lendin' me something to wear after my swim this mornin'."

Jolee laughed. "Ya got Pax's attention at breakfast, I'll tell ya that for sure!"

"He's . . . a different sort of man," Rivers remarked.

"My brother? Oh, yes! Different . . . that's a nice way of puttin' it. Oh, just 'cause I'm his sister doesn't mean I don't know how handsome he is. All women do. But he's a handful all right. I know how to deal with him 'cause I've grown up with him. But he can be a real pickle."

"I can see that," Rivers said, unable to keep from smiling.

"Now, me . . . I'm sweet on Weston Warner. You met him tonight. The one that's near as tall as Pax."

Rivers peered through the window and into the kitchen. She had noticed the way Jolee looked at that one. Weston Warner was a handsome man. Though lacking the unusually magnetic look of Paxton, he was also dark-haired. He had brown eyes and seemed a nice fellow.

"So . . . he's your beau?" Rivers commented.

Jolee laughed. "Weston? Darlin', Weston Warner doesn't know I'm alive! I'm Paxton's little sister, and that's all I've ever been to him."

Rivers looked at Jolee in disbelief. "You're teasin' me."

Jolee shook her head. "Nope. I just don't catch his eye. Oh, believe me, I've tried. But I guess I'm just not what he's lookin' for."

"Is that why you're not married yet? Because you've liked him for so long?"

Jolee hesitated. "You're as sharp as my best kitchen knife, Rivers Brighton. Yes, that's why. I can't get that man out of my heart and mind long enough to consider anybody else."

Rivers was silent for a moment. She listened to the creaking of the swing as it moved back and forth, to and fro. Then she asked, "Is that why Paxton isn't married too? Some girl has had his attention for too long?"

Jolee looked at Rivers. Her eyes were serious and her mouth showed no trace of the smile that was ever present there.

• • •

"In a manner of speakin'," Jolee answered. Her mind was awhirl. Should she answer the girl's question with complete and unbridled honesty? Should she relate the story to her? Paxton would have a fit if he ever found out she'd told Rivers. Jolee knew that for certain. With a deep breath she made her choice.

"Ruby Catherine Dupree. That's her name."

Rivers sensed an odd twitching begin in her stomach at Jolee's revelation.

Jolee continued, "She was very lovely. All the men and boys 'round here admired her. But, as so often goes, the two most beautiful people in the county found each other. Paxton thought he was plum gone on Ruby, and she worshipped the ground he walked on. Everyone talked about what beautiful children they would have. She had the lightest blue eyes I had ever seen and pure butter-blonde hair."

Jolee stopped for a moment. Rivers peered through the window once again, this time at Paxton. He was smiling and talking to his friends, completely unaware of the conversation going on out on the front porch.

"Did she die?" Rivers asked. After all, Jolee had spoken of her in the past tense.

"No. They were engaged to be married, Paxton and Ruby. And then one mornin' . . . 'bout two

42

weeks before the wedding . . . she was gone. Her family moved away in the middle of the night. No one heard from them. Paxton knows, though. I'm sure Paxton knows why they left."

"And he never heard from her again?"

"Nope. Not that I know of."

A chill traveled through Rivers's body, and she shivered involuntarily. There was something unspoken in Jolee's story. Something ominous and unpleasant.

"It's getting chilly out. Let's go in and go to bed, what do ya say?" Jolee suggested.

Rivers nodded, although she hated the idea of having to walk past the men. No doubt by now they all knew her story.

As the women entered, all the men stood up, and Paxton said, "You ain't turnin' in already, are ya, Jo?"

"Some of us enjoy a good night's rest. Especially before the Sabbath," Jolee teased.

"It sure was nice meetin' you, Miss Brighton," one of the men said, smiling at Rivers.

She nodded and tried to force a friendly smile.

"Yes. We're glad to hear you've come to visit Jolee and help her with this mean ol' cuss," Weston Warner added.

Rivers looked to Paxton. He knew she was looking at him but did not return her gaze.

Instead he said, "I told the boys how plum tickled Jo was when ya wrote and said ya were comin' for a long visit." Then his eyes did meet hers and he added, "And how glad we are to have ya here." The intense blue in his eyes caused Rivers's heart to leap.

She looked away quickly, unable to meet the piercing stare.

"Did my dear brother mention my friend Rivers don't much put up with his vinegar? She poured a cup of milk in his lap at breakfast this mornin' and half drowned him in the creek to boot!" Jolee teased.

"Now, dang it all, Jo! Don't go tellin' the boys things like that," Paxton pled as he squeezed his eyes shut for a moment in a humiliated grimace. "She's exaggeratin', boys. Don't listen to little sis," Paxton chuckled, turning back to study the cards in his hand.

"Well, good night, boys. You all be good now," Jolee called over her shoulder as she walked toward her room.

Rivers followed, catching wisps of the conversation behind them.

"She's a quiet one," someone said.

"Oh, don't let her fool ya, boys. She's tough as an old cowhide," Paxton answered.

◆◆◆◆◆

That night, Rivers dreamt of trains—of fast, rushing air and the smell of boxcars. Of rain and storms frocked with thunder, lightning, and the sounds trains make as they travel over wet tracks.

Ever present in those dreams, however, like a ghostly visitor watching her, was the disturbing and handsome figure of Paxton Gray.

Ruby would never have pulled him in the creek, Paxton thought as he lay in bed after a long night of cards with the boys. Ruby was frail and beautiful and knew her manners. He closed his eyes and tried to envision her. But that danged girl kept coming into his mind instead. He had sworn to himself he had learned his life's lesson at the hand of Ruby Dupree. He had done what he knew to be right and look how it had turned out. Nope. No female would have a chance to blame Paxton Gray for heartbreak again.

Still, Rivers had looked as delicious as fresh cherry pie when she came walking out of Jolee's room in that dress, her hair braided after cleaning up from her dip in the creek that morning. For the first time in his life, Paxton felt his mouth literally begin to water at the sight of a girl. As pretty as Ruby was, his mouth had never watered when he'd looked at her. He told himself it was because he had missed a good breakfast, that's all. Didn't his morning milk end up in his lap?

He couldn't help chuckling to himself at the thought of that girl pouring milk in his lap. He liked her for it! She wasn't gonna let anybody treat her badly—something to be admired in a person. He turned over and was soon sound asleep.

CHAPTER FOUR

"Wash the beans, stem the beans, snap the beans. Shell the peas, wash the peas. Does it ever end?" Rivers asked Jolee as they each collapsed into a kitchen chair.

"Oh, eventually," Jolee sighed. "But it's a pretty sight, isn't it? Rows and rows of jars bottled up with vegetables for the winter months."

Rivers nodded. They were lovely. She felt an overwhelming sense of accomplishment at the sight of the preserved food. She had helped Jolee cut her bean and pea putting-up time in half, at least. Besides, she and Jolee had become good friends over the past few weeks. Rivers no longer felt like an intruder at the Gray farm. She knew Jolee wanted her there, even if Paxton was averse to it. And she had a plan—a bit of mischief swarming around in her mind where Jolee and Weston Warner were concerned. She had watched Jolee when Weston was around, and she knew that, although her friend talked lightly of her attraction for the man, Jolee was deeply in love with him. Rivers had stayed on at the Gray farm for one reason alone—to repay Jolee's kindness to her.

Yet that reason for staying, she whispered to herself, was a lie, and deep within her she knew

46

it. Certainly she wanted to see Jolee happy. But the truth was Rivers was finding it increasingly difficult to think of leaving Paxton, even though she knew he held her in no great esteem whatsoever. He was addictive somehow. She found herself waking up in the morning drenched in a sort of desperation—a need to see him as soon as she could. She thought of him almost constantly, thrilled at the simplest touch or attention from him. Her fascination with Paxton Gray was dangerous, and she knew it. Yet she couldn't help it! She couldn't give the sight of him up! In truth, Paxton was the thing keeping Rivers from running to the tracks and hopping a train to escape the odd aching in her heart, the longing to be of value to him.

Thus Rivers had settled into a happy routine of farm life. Through Jolee, she felt at home, welcome, and not the least bit indebted. She knew Jolee enjoyed having her there, whether or not Paxton did. Most of the time, Paxton simply seemed indifferent to Rivers's presence at the farm—seemed no more interested in her than he did the sacks of potatoes in the root cellar.

As Rivers sat reflecting on the past weeks, she and Jolee both startled at a knock on the front door.

"Let me see who it is, Jo," Rivers said, rising and walking through the parlor. "You just sit there and rest."

"Hey there, Rivers," Weston Warner greeted as Rivers opened the door.

"Hello, Weston. What brings you out this way?" Rivers asked as she stepped aside to let him enter.

"I'm lookin' for Pax. He around?" Weston asked.

"Jo . . . it's Weston," Rivers said. She smiled as Jolee appeared a moment later, a scarlet blush of delight warming her cheeks.

"I'm lookin' for Pax, Jo," Weston said, removing his hat and smiling at Jolee. "Seen him 'round anywhere?"

Jolee walked over to them, and Rivers could see her friend was all too aware of her peas-stained apron and the strand of hair escaping from her braid.

"Um . . ." Jolee stammered, trying to tuck the strand of loose hair behind her ear, "I think he's in the barn fixin' one of the stalls."

Rivers smiled at the amused grin spreading across Weston's face as he looked Jolee up and down.

"Been cannin' this mornin', Jo?" he asked.

"Beans and peas," Jolee answered.

It never ceased to amaze Rivers how tongue-tied Jolee became when Weston entered a room.

"You all will have to invite me for supper some time and let a neighbor sample 'em for ya," Weston coaxed.

Rivers quickly looked to Jolee, but the girl only stood smiling. She couldn't believe it! Jolee didn't seem to notice the insinuation Weston was hurling at her.

"Tonight would be a good night, wouldn't it, Jo? You come on over for supper tonight, Weston. We've just taken a couple of cherry pies out of the oven," Rivers said, winking at her friend.

"Oh! Oh, yes! Tonight. Tonight would be a good night, Weston. For you to come to supper, I mean," Jolee stammered.

"Well now, that's just fine. But a man practically has to invite himself." Weston smiled and asked, "Now, ya say Pax's out in the barn?"

Jolee nodded.

"All right then. I guess I'll be by about . . ." Weston coaxed again, motioning with one hand for Jolee to finish his sentence.

"Oh! Um . . . Five. Five should be about right," Jolee stammered.

"Well, you ladies have a nice day now," Weston offered, tipping his hat to Jolee and then Rivers.

"You too," Jolee called as he sauntered across the front porch.

When Weston was well out of earshot, Rivers exclaimed, "Jolee Gray! I swear you're as dumb as an ox when he's around! He's gonna think you're not interested."

Jolee rubbed her forehead with one hand. "He

just makes me so nervous, Rivers! I can't help it. Did ya see the way he was lookin' at me? I know he just thought I was the plainest thing on earth. I mean, look at me. All covered in preservin' mess, hair flyin' every which way . . ."

"And a smushed pea spot on the tip of your nose," Rivers added with a giggle.

"Oh fine, Rivers. I feel much better now, thank you," Jolee exclaimed, brushing the evidence of having been canning from her nose and turning back to the kitchen.

"You're beautiful that way. I don't doubt he was standin' there thinkin' what a cute little wife and mother you'd be," Rivers said.

"Oh, of course, Rivers. I'm sure that's just what he was thinkin'," Jolee sighed.

"I don't care what you say, Jolee. Weston Warner likes you. I think he's liked you for a long time but doesn't know how to go about startin' up with you," Rivers announced, following her into the kitchen.

"Well now, I'm certain you're right!" Jolee agreed, her tone and smile thick with sarcasm. "In fact, I'm sure he's just itchin' to take me in his arms and smother me with kisses! It's all in the way he ignores me most of the time."

"Yes. It is."

Jolee sighed with exasperation. "All right, all right. Enough silly talk. Let's get these pies to coolin' outside."

• • •

"Hey there, Pax," Weston greeted as he entered the barn. "I finally got myself invited to supper at your house!"

Paxton stopped hammering and looked up. "No! You're foolin' me. She asked ya to supper?" he asked, disbelieving.

Weston nodded. "Course . . . your little friend helped her out a bit. Come to think of it, maybe Jo didn't really want me comin' for supper." A frown wrinkled his brow.

"No siree. She wants ya for supper. She swore me to secrecy and to not be invitin' ya my own self. She just don't know how to go about askin', that's all. Ya make her all jumpy and nervous," Paxton stated.

"Oh, I'm sure that ain't true at all," Weston mumbled. "What ya doin' to that stall?"

Paxton looked back at his project. "Snort kicked it down the other day when I was cleanin' somethin' out of his hoof. He's an ornery ol' boy." Paxton looked back to his friend. "So are ya or aren't ya ever gonna get around to bein' my brother-in-law?"

Weston laughed. "We'll see, Pax. What about you? You're near as old as I am. Ain't you plannin' to settle down into family life?"

Paxton chuckled and shook his head. "Not me. No sir. I ain't cut out for bein' a good husband and daddy. I'll leave that up to purty boys like you."

"Seems to me ya thought ya were cut out for it once before," Weston mumbled in a low, serious tone.

Paxton paused before answering. "Yeah? Well, I wasn't thinkin' straight back then."

Weston looked back toward the house. "Seems to me that friend of Jolee's is plum intoxicatin' to look at. And she's spunky to boot."

"Oh, she's spunky all right. A might too big for her own britches, if ya ask me. She got her dander up at me the other day, and we went around for awhile," Paxton admitted with a chuckle.

"Did you end up on your seat in the crick again?" Weston asked.

"Nope," Paxton answered. "But yesterday mornin' . . . I found the fly in my flannels was sewed shut. I discovered it at a right awkward time, mind you. Weren't a convenient moment to have my fly sewed shut. Had to strip down to nothin' just to take care of my business."

Weston broke into roaring laughter. "You're joshin' me, boy! She sewed up your fly?"

Paxton nodded and laughed himself. "I was near to red-faced anger at first. But after a minute, well . . . I thought it was dang clever."

"Well, I don't doubt for a second ya didn't deserve it. And don't go feedin' me them oats about not bein' cut out for settlin' down. I know ya better than you'd like me to, Paxton Gray."

Paxton chuckled again. "Yeah, I suppose ya do at that."

◆ ◆ ◆ ◆ ◆

"Settle down, Jolee. You look beautiful! Just beautiful," Rivers encouraged.

"What if the beef is too tough, Rivers? He'll think I can't boil water!" Jolee cried in a whisper.

"The beef will be just fine, Jo. Now, take a deep breath and calm down before he gets here to find you pantin' at him," Rivers whispered with a giggle.

Jolee took a deep breath. "All right. I'm fine now. I'm fine," she whispered.

There was a knock on the front door, and Jolee jumped. "I'm sick to my stomach, Rivers! I can't answer it. I mean, if a man hates a woman's cookin' . . . well, there just ain't no other reason to like her then."

Rivers took her friend's hand and pulled her toward the parlor. "Just open the door and say hello," she whispered.

But at the very moment Rivers pushed her friend forward to open the door, Weston Warner stepped through it and into the house. Rivers gasped and her hands flew to her mouth as she saw Jolee go stumbling straight into Weston's arms.

"Ya all right?" Weston asked as he steadied Jolee.

"Yes. Fine. Thank you," Jolee stammered, shooting a threatening stare at Rivers and smoothing her apron. "Come on in . . . supper's almost ready. I'll just call Pax in."

"I'll fetch him," Rivers volunteered, dashing past them and out the front door. She quickly walked to the barn and called, "Paxton? Weston's here, and Jolee's ready to sit down to supper. You better look like bein' prompt. I've already messed up his welcome."

Paxton turned and smiled. "She's nervous, is she?" he asked.

"As a fresh spring bunny," Rivers whispered, momentarily unnerved by the piercing blue directed at her. "And to make it worse, I gave her a little shove toward the door . . . you know, so she would actually let him in the house, and she went flyin' right into his arms!"

Paxton smiled. "Good. They both need a little shove here and there."

He walked past her and toward the house. Rivers paused. She felt depressed suddenly. Watching Paxton walk toward the house, she realized if things did work out between Weston and Jolee, which she had no doubt they would, she would have to leave. She would no longer be able to stay.

Paxton turned and looked at her. "Well, are ya gonna stand there gawkin' at my fine fanny . . . or what?"

Rivers clenched her teeth. "I am not lookin' at your . . . your behind," she growled.

"Then come on. I'm starvin' half to death," he said, winking at her.

♦ ♦ ♦ ♦ ♦

Supper was delicious, and Paxton made sure Weston and Jolee talked a great deal to each other. When they'd eaten, Rivers began to help clear the dishes.

"Let me do that," Weston said with a wink at Rivers. "I'll help ya get 'em all done up, Jo. It's the least I can do after such a fine meal," he offered.

"Oh, no. You don't have to . . ." Jolee began.

"Why sure I do! I gotta show my appreciation, now don't I?" Weston assured her.

"And I um . . . I . . . uh . . ." Paxton began. He looked at Rivers and continued, "Um . . . I gotta get to finishin' that stall in the barn. I'll be back in a while."

"But I thought you . . ." Rivers began.

Paxton took hold of her arm quickly, "You're right. I do need your help out there. Come on." He began pulling her with him toward the back door.

Once outside, Rivers said, "Could you have been just a bit more obvious?"

"Most likely not," he admitted, letting go of her. He stopped, inhaling a deep breath. Sighing, he looked around seeming unusually content.

"It's still light. Let's go down to the pond and skip rocks or somethin'."

Rivers raised her eyebrows. She couldn't believe her ears. "Skip rocks?" she asked.

"Sure! We'll make a game of it. My best is seven. What do you wanna bet?" he asked.

She followed him as he walked down the sloping north pasture toward the pond. "I don't think I had better gamble with you. Seven is pretty impressive."

"I only did it once. I guess I do about five on a good skippin' day."

Rivers smiled. "You're serious," she stated.

He stopped and looked down at her. "Of course I am."

"I didn't think you wasted a moment of your precious time."

"It ain't a waste. It's relaxin'. Keeps ya from gettin' too all-fired uptight and worried," Paxton explained, continuing on toward the pond.

Several minutes later, Rivers found herself at the pond in the sole company of Paxton Gray. And she was anxious. Never, since the moment he'd dropped her in the tub several weeks before, had Rivers been so secluded in his company.

As she watched him studying the ground around the edge of the pond, her heart began to beat a little quicker as he dipped one hand into the water, rubbing the back of his neck with the moisture. He stooped and picked up several rocks, looking at them carefully, and slipping one in particular into his pocket.

"All right, now. I'll go first," he said.

Rivers smiled and watched as he threw his first skipper. Splish, splish, splish. Three skips.

"Dang. Not flat enough. All right . . . you go," Paxton encouraged, turning to Rivers.

She still thought he was joking. Paxton Gray? The worst workhorse in three counties, skipping rocks in the pond? It just didn't seem real.

Rivers bent down and picked up several rocks. She found a good, flat, smooth one. Splish, splish, splish, splish. Four skips.

"Not bad. Not bad at all," Paxton said. "For a fly sewer."

Rivers wrinkled her nose at him, and he chuckled. "Let's make this more interestin'," he said. "You win . . . and I do anything ya say. I win . . . you do what I say," he bartered, chuckling.

"Not me! You'll want me to shovel out the horse stalls for a month, or somethin' the like," Rivers confirmed, shaking her head.

"Now, hang on. Just hang on," he muttered, thoughtful for a moment. "Okay then. Let's say it has to be done right here, right now. Say somethin' like . . . I'll play your favorite tune on my harmonica. Or iron all your petticoats. Somethin' like that."

"You play the harmonica?" Rivers asked, suddenly intrigued.

"You bet. Deal?" Paxton asked, extending a hand toward her.

Rivers narrowed her eyes and suspiciously looked at him. "Show me the harmonica first," she said.

"You callin' me a liar?" he asked, smiling and reaching into the front pocket of his trousers and producing a harmonica.

Rivers raised her eyebrows in astonishment. She then took his hand and shook it firmly. "Deal, then," she agreed.

"All right. Let's get to goin' here." Paxton chuckled and threw his next rock.

Rivers judged they must have skipped rocks for half an hour, laughing abundantly and heckling each other.

Finally, Paxton said, "All right. Last skip." And he tossed his rock. It made seven ripples in the water, and he clapped. "Beat that," he said, triumphantly crossing his muscular arms across his impressive chest.

Rivers defiantly looked at him, kissed the rock she held in her hand for luck, and threw it.

"Eight! I skipped an eight! I win!" she giggled.

"I guess you do at that," Paxton admitted, as a sly grin spread across his fabulous face. "All right. I'm as good as my word. What will it be? Ironin'?"

"Harmonica," Rivers reminded. She had always loved the harmonica. Her grandfather had played one. As a child, she sat for hours, listening to him play and never once tiring of it.

"Has to be somethin' I've at least heard of now," Paxton said as he patted the instrument in the palm of his hand.

"All right . . . um . . . how about 'Beautiful Brown Eyes,'" she suggested. "My daddy used to sing that to me when we were travelin'."

He raised his eyebrows. "All right." And in the next moment, Paxton Gray began to play the melancholy tune.

Rivers felt goose bumps rising on her arms and neck. He played beautifully! The harmonica sang into the warm evening air, and she watched completely mesmerized as Paxton's mouth coaxed the harmonica into producing the perfectly played tune. She grimaced only once, but it was not for the sake of an ill-played note. For each note of the melody was as clear as new glass. It was the uncomfortable and sudden painful pang stabbing her heart as she watched him that caused a frown to wrinkle her forehead for a moment. What a perfect man he was, she thought. Oh, not literally. No one was perfect, after all. But he was to her. Even with his quick temper and pride, he was wonderful. Beautiful, hardworking, and funny. How could she ever leave the farm and not sorrowfully pine away after him for the rest of her life?

When he finished, he smiled. "Ya like that."

He stated it, for Rivers knew her pleasure was obvious on her face.

"Yes. Thank you," she admitted, sighing contentedly.

"All right then . . . double or nothin'?" he asked with a grin.

"You think you can beat my eight?" Rivers giggled.

"Oh, I'm willin' to give it a try," he chuckled.

"All right. Double or nothin'," she said.

Rivers began looking for an appropriate rock and found one perfectly shaped for skipping. Smiling at him, she sent the rock flying across the water. "Eight, again!" she squealed with delight.

A mischievous smile spread across Paxton's handsome face. He winked at Rivers and reached into his pocket, producing the rock he'd put there when they'd first started. She had forgotten about his putting the rock into his pocket and now wondered why he hadn't used it before.

"Double or nothin'," he reminded her.

Rivers smiled confidently at him. Eight skips was impossible to beat. But she watched in utter amazement as Paxton sent the rock skipping lightly across the water, her mouth dropping open as she turned to look at him, stunned.

"I counted at least eleven. Didn't you?" he asked, quirking one brow.

"You're either terribly lucky . . . or else you've been foolin' me all along," Rivers accused.

Paxton just smiled. "See that tree right back there?" he asked.

Rivers turned and looked at the willow tree standing a ways from them. "Yes."

"Come on," he said, motioning for her to follow him.

Rivers followed, although tentative, anxious somehow. Rivers followed as Paxton ducked under the lower, drooping branches of the willow and stood beneath the tree. He took her by the shoulders, pushing her back against the large trunk.

"Double or nothin'," he reminded in a low, mesmerizing mumble.

Rivers straightened and tried to look unruffled. The truth was her heart was beating so violently she feared she might actually drop dead at his feet.

"What are you doin'?" she asked.

"Oh, nothin' too awful bad. Just plannin' on stealin' a kiss. Two actually. Double or nothin', you remember," Paxton answered, winking at her.

Rivers giggled nervously. "Oh! I see. You're just teasin' me," she said. He was quite a tease. She had learned it was often hard to tell whether the man was serious or not.

Paxton shook his head. "Nope. I figure bein' able to make a rock skip eleven times oughta earn me somethin'." His smile faded then. "You ain't too awful sure how to take me sometimes, are ya, Rivers?" he asked.

She didn't answer, for it was the first time in the three weeks since she'd arrived that he'd used her name. It was an overpowering emotion—the thrill of hearing him utter it. Besides, she was aware Paxton knew he was right. She wasn't at all sure how to handle him most of the time.

"Well, I figure . . . if I steal a kiss from ya once . . . you'll herd me in there as a plain, regular sort of feller and won't be so jumpy whenever I'm around. I mean, you'll see I've got my own weaknesses when it comes to a purty girl, right? Now, hold still," he ordered. Rivers fancied the teasing manner was suddenly absent from his voice.

Trying to take a step back, Rivers bumped solidly into the tree as Paxton's head descended toward hers. Her heart still pounded brutally as she realized he was undaunted. He reached up and planted his hands firmly on the tree branches at either side of her head, and instinctively her mind told her to run. To escape before her heart would be lost forever. But her hands reached back and held the trunk of the tree, steadying her trembling body. Rivers closed her eyes when at last his face was too close for her to focus on it clearly. She felt his lips brush her cheek lightly.

• • •

Paxton firmly gripped the tree branches. He had to move ahead slowly. He could sense Rivers was like a scared rabbit, ready to bolt and run at the slightest sign of threat. He wouldn't reach out and pull her into his arms like he wanted to. He just wanted to taste her kiss once. Those cherry-red lips had been tempting him since the first time he'd seen them clearly that night in the barn, when her true identity had been revealed to him in the lamplight. And so, the tree bark scratched his fingers and palms as he tightened his hold on the limbs.

Rivers perceived a sort of thrilling fear begin to rise within her at his kissing her cheek. Paxton frightened her—frightened her because the sight of him was like gazing into a dream. He was the exemplary vision of a man. She sensed the passion he was capable of generating would be overpowering in the very least. But she wouldn't run from him. She'd dreamt of this since the first moment she'd laid eyes on him, and she wouldn't run from it.

Paxton kissed her cheek softly a second time and moved his body closer to hers, keeping his hands on the tree. The fragrance of her skin was unlike anything he'd ever experienced, and it refreshed him—like the cool morning breeze in autumn. He let his cheek brush hers and took a deep breath. Then, turning his head slightly, he sampled for the first time the sweetness of her delicate, velvet-soft mouth.

Rivers's knees began to fail her. They buckled entirely when Paxton's mouth flirted with her own. He ably caught her in his arms, however, and pulled her to him, never breaking the seal of their lips. Rivers found herself oddly short of breath and turned her head from him. Paxton took her chin in his hand and brought her face to meet his once more. She looked up into Paxton's eyes for only a moment before they narrowed as he kissed her again. The blue of his eyes was mesmerizing in their near translucence, and as he kissed her this time, she knew he watched her, and she began to tremble. The power of his kiss coupled with the intensity of his narrowed stare stole Rivers's confidence from her. She wondered what he thought of her, if he enjoyed kissing her and the taste on her lips. She was intensely aware of the scent of him—of his whiskers as they scratched the tender flesh around her mouth—of the power contained in the muscles of his chest and arms. She knew she would feel ashamed for it later, but finally, closing her eyes, she let her arms slide around his waist and returned his powerful, moist, delicious kisses.

Time evaded Rivers's senses, and she had no

idea how much had passed when he broke their kiss and rested his forehead against her own briefly.

He whispered, "Consider my winnin's as paid."

Paxton's own mind and senses were a tornado of emotion. This confirmed it. He had to lock himself away from her inwardly. She was, indeed, dangerous to the way of life he'd come to accept. And he didn't want that life to alter. He'd worked far too hard to achieve it. He had nobody to be responsible for, no one to worry about but himself and Jolee. And he was certain his sister would soon marry Weston and leave him to his own chosen solitude.

Paxton released Rivers and tucked his shirt tail into his trousers. "Well . . . guess we oughta be headin' back in now. They've had long enough to get over bein' bashful with each other."

"Yes." Rivers cleared her throat, trying to act as unaffected as he did. She took several steps toward the house before her knees gave way from the lingering effects of his kissing her, her body enveloped numbingly in goose bumps.

"Whoops! Watch out now," he warned, lunging forward and catching hold of her arm to steady her.

"Gopher hole," she lied. "Better watch your step. It's so dark now."

• • •

When Rivers and Paxton entered the house, it was to be greeted by Jolee's and Weston's beaming, smiling faces.

"We've finished the dishes while you two were out . . . doin' whatever it was you were doin'," Weston announced.

"Fixin' the stall," Paxton informed him, grinning mischievously.

"It oughta be right sturdy by now," Weston added.

Rivers was all too aware of the understanding winks passing quickly between the two men.

"Let's all sit down in the parlor. Do ya have time, Weston?" Jolee asked.

Even the beaming smile radiating from the sweet face of her friend couldn't erase the euphoric feelings and thoughts bouncing around inside Rivers's mind and body. She could still feel Paxton's breath on her cheek, his arms around her, his firm chest crushing against her. She could still taste the warm flavor of his mouth.

"Where were ya all anyhow?" Weston asked innocently as they all took seats in the parlor. Rivers knew she blushed and hoped with all her heart it was too dark in the room for anyone to notice.

"Same as you," Paxton said.

"What?" Jolee exclaimed, and Rivers noticed

the blush on her face as well. "I mean," Jolee continued, "dishes?"

"No, Jo," Paxton chuckled knowingly. "Playin' in the water. We were down at the pond skippin' rocks."

"I hope he warned ya 'forehand, Rivers," Weston said, smiling.

"Of what?" Rivers asked, curious.

"That he can skip a rock at least twelve times 'cross the pond if'n he has the mind to," Weston answered.

"No, he didn't," Rivers said, glaring at Paxton, who only shrugged his broad shoulders.

"I let her win once," Paxton chuckled. "Played my harmonica for her."

"You didn't! He's lyin', Rivers! He don't play for nobody!" Weston exclaimed.

"He plays beautifully," Rivers stated truthfully, as humiliation at his toying with her began to course through her veins.

"Beautifully?" Paxton questioned, as his voice went high and squeaky with disgust. "Good, maybe. Perfectly, even. But, 'beautifully'? Only kind of men that do things 'beautifully' is the same kind that uses curlin' rods in their hair."

"He must be takin' to you all right then, Rivers," Jolee remarked. "He doesn't play for anybody but himself and the stock usually."

"I guess I'm at least as privileged as the stock then," Rivers said.

"Don't get too all confident there, girl," Paxton chuckled.

Rivers glared at Paxton and stuck her tongue out at him quickly. She was instantly horrified as he winked at her, licking his lips with insinuation. He chuckled and shook his head, satisfied at having obviously unsettled her.

Rivers glanced at Jolee, who was too involved in her quiet conversation with Weston to have noticed her brother's shameless flirting. And Rivers was thankful for it.

◆◆◆◆◆

The four sat talking for nearly two more hours before Weston finally stood to take his leave.

"That was the finest meal I've ever had, Jolee," Weston said, taking one of her hands and pressing it between his own. "I hope you'll be askin' me over again soon." He smiled at her and tipped his hat to Paxton and Rivers.

"Thank ya for comin'," Jolee called as he walked out the front door.

Paxton stood smiling at his sister, and she blushed as she turned and saw him staring at her.

"What are you grinnin' at, Pax?" she asked shortly as she moved past him and into the kitchen.

"Oh, nothin'. Nothin' at all, Jo," he said chuckling. "Just that you're glowin' like a fire-bug in the summer dark! Did he give ya a big lickery kiss while ya were doin' up the dishes?"

68

Jolee's mouth dropped open as she turned to scold him. "No! Of course not! He's a gentleman, Paxton. Course you wouldn't understand that," she teased. "And anyway, what were you all doin' out by the pond? Skippin' rocks? That's about the dumbest story you've ever come up with, Pax," Jolee snapped.

"Ain't no story, Jo. It's the truth, ain't it, girl?" he said, turning to Rivers.

"Yes," she answered shortly.

Rivers felt the hurt and humiliation deepening at the siblings' light treatment of what she considered a very serious situation. Without a word, she turned and walked toward her room.

"Hey. Aren't ya gonna say good night?" Paxton asked as he caught hold of her arm just outside her bedroom.

"Good night," she snapped, wrenching her arm free of his grasp.

"Hold on. Hold on. I'm sorry. I shouldn't have teased ya that way. I just . . ." Paxton began in a hushed voice.

"Teased me? You weren't teasin' me. Don't think I'm stupid enough to believe it was just a friendly teasin'. Men. You're all so . . . that's what women are here for, aren't we? For you to humiliate, to enable you to make yourselves feel superior and powerful?" Rivers accused in a whisper, glancing toward the kitchen to ensure that Jolee couldn't hear her.

The frown capturing Paxton's face was complete. Not just eyebrows and forehead, but also mouth, eyes, and jaw. Rivers was at once incredibly uncomfortable. Yet she wanted to reach up and entangle her fingers in the soft, sable-colored waves hanging at his forehead. She wanted his kiss on her mouth again. What had happened? The moments at the pond under the tree had changed things. She would never be able to leave him now.

"Yep. That's it, all right," he growled. And before she could think to escape, he pulled her brutally against his body and nearly smothered her with his hard, angry kiss.

Rivers knew he meant for it to hurt her—to make her feel as if he were using her mouth for the sheer pleasure of his own. Even so, something in his kiss thrilled her. She sensed it wasn't fully as cruel as he intended it to be.

"You're exactly right," he growled after breaking from her. "In fact, since you're on to me now . . . I guess I'll have to satisfy my manly needs somewhere else." He stormed across the hall to his own room, slamming the door behind him.

Rivers scolded herself as she climbed into bed. Jolee had told her weeks ago about Ruby. No doubt memories of her were the reasons Paxton took what Rivers had accused him of so fully to heart. Paxton was a tease! That's all it was. He

70

hadn't meant to hurt her feelings out under the willow. He'd only been playing with her—a friendly flirtatious playfulness.

Rivers tossed and turned and was utterly guilt-ridden for at least an hour. Sleep evaded her guilty conscience to the point she was driven to put it to rest. Quietly she crept from her room and put her ear to the door of Paxton's room across the way. A light shone from the crack at the bottom of the door, and she could hear his bed squeaking. She swallowed hard, mustering every bit of courage she could, and without knocking opened the door and entered his room.

"Before you throw me out . . . I've come to apologize," she blurted out. "I . . ." She couldn't finish her sentence as she looked up at him then. Paxton was sitting on the bed in nothing but a towel, having obviously just finished bathing.

"Oh, I'm sorry," she stammered. "I . . . I'll come back later. I had no idea . . ."

"Naw. You go on ahead and say your piece now. We'll both sleep better," he grumbled, standing and walking toward her, gripping the towel firmly at his waist.

The surprise of finding him in such a state had swept all coherent thought from Rivers's mind. What had she planned to say? It was gone—every word of it.

"Yeah? So?" Paxton coaxed as he stood directly in front of her.

There were still beads of water covering his chest, arms, and shoulders. As Rivers's eyes wandered a fraction, she noted his stomach, too, was still damp. "I . . . um . . ." she still couldn't organize her thinking into words.

"I'm sorry," Paxton seemed to finish for her. "I was only teasin' ya, Rivers," he whispered as a grin broke across his handsome face.

"I know," she said, casting her gaze downward. "I guess I was just tired out or somethin'."

"Yep. My kisses can have that effect on some women," he chuckled.

She looked up ready to do battle, but smiled, relieved as she saw the twinkling mirth in his eyes. "I don't think you're as tough as you like to pretend," she whispered.

He smiled. "Ya got me by the gills there, girl." He lowered his voice again and whispered, "Tell ya what. Double or nothin'."

She rolled her eyes and sighed heavily. "I've learned my lesson about bettin' with you, Paxton Gray."

"Now, just hear me out. Double or nothin' . . . you let me kiss ya one more time, to make up for that mean thing I did in the hallway earlier, and I won't go teasin' ya beyond what ya can handle any more. Deal?"

Rivers looked up into his dazzling smile. She shook her head nervously. "No, no, no. That's all right. I understand. Really, I do. I provoked you before." She began to back away.

He ignored her answer and reaching out took hold of her arm. As his head descended toward hers, he whispered, "I just wanna make sure ya know there's somethin' besides playin' the harmonica that I do 'beautifully.' Even if I don't use curlin' rods in my hair."

Then Paxton's lips touched hers so tenderly that if it hadn't have been for the pure tremor of titillation moving through her like thunder echoing in a mountain valley, she wouldn't have felt his kiss at all.

He gently pulled her into his arms. The beads of water still clinging to his body united with the warmth of his skin, moistening her nightdress like a hot, sweet, summer cloud burst.

His mouth began discovering hers once more. Now, the uncompromising, powerful, thrilling kisses they had shared under the sweeping boughs of the willow returned. Rivers was bound helplessly in the confusing yet ecstatic thrill the feel of his mouth toying with her own sent resounding through her.

"Now," he whispered as his body seemed to unwillingly separate itself from hers. "I clean forgot to keep hold of my towel. So, unless you're wantin' to see me bare neked . . . ya better . . ."

Rivers gasped and, without waiting for him to finish his sentence, turned and fled across the hall to her own room. She could hear his mischievous chuckle as he closed the door behind her.

Climbing back into her own bed, a contented smile donned her beautiful cherried mouth. The knowledge he had forgiven her the cruel words she'd spat at him earlier sent her off to a peaceful, if somewhat dreamy slumber—dreams dominated by the perfect kisses of the man who, in fact, held her heart captive.

CHAPTER FIVE

After the night Weston Warner came to supper, Jolee lost some of the extreme nervousness that had previously enveloped her in his presence. Weston spent more of his time visiting with Jolee when he dropped by now and again and even escorted her to one of the church socials in town.

Yet as Rivers watched Weston and Jolee becoming more familiar, her own anxieties deepened. She knew she could no longer stay in the Gray home once Jolee married Weston and moved to his farm, as she had no doubt she would. But returning to her grandparents seemed a dismal prospect. Furthermore, Rivers knew she could not continue to hop boxcars from town to town, living the existence of a drifter. She'd grown beyond posing as a young boy to find work—grown beyond the lonely, unsafe life of an orphaned girl. She was a woman and longed for a home, a life, to be loved and to love in return.

Trying to push the necessity of leaving to the back of her mind, Rivers attempted to go about her existence each day happy for Jolee and Weston and yet selfishly hoping their engagement, when it was announced, would be a long one.

Rivers tried in vain to push other thoughts to the dark recesses of her mind too. Thoughts of a strong, handsome, untouchable man whose kisses still burned through her memory! Paxton had become increasingly less friendly. Ever since the night Weston had come for supper, the night she and Paxton had shared such intimate moments, he seemed to withdraw into an impenetrable hull. He smiled seldom, talked even less, and seemed to wear a perpetual frown across his brow. Rivers knew he'd regretted his flirting with her. He rarely met her eye to eye, and he was brief in his conversation with her. He was polite to everyone, even to Rivers—coolly polite. Still, Rivers sensed his discomfort with her.

Several times, she'd tried to find the courage to leave them, these people she was in love with. But each time, the now-fading courage that had carried her through so many of life's trying situations abandoned her completely. Often at night, she'd hear the distant rumble of the train on the tracks and listen to its mournful whistle seeming to warn her, calling to her. But each time she let the train echo into the distance without an attempt at joining its journey.

And then, Jolee was bitten. The horrible guilt Rivers felt toward the incident, coupled with Jolee's need for help, kept her from leaving when she came closest to finding the will to do so.

◆ ◆ ◆ ◆ ◆

For Rivers, the events of the day Jolee was bitten began with an unpleasant interaction with

Paxton. As she stepped out of the house on her way to the barn, Rivers's shoe caught on a loose front porch board. Consequently, she stumbled, landing on her hands and knees, a painful splinter puncturing the palm of her hand, burying itself under her flesh.

"Ow!" Rivers exclaimed. Sitting down promptly on her behind, she studied the large sliver of wood imbedded in her palm.

"Let me see it," Paxton growled, as he mounted the front porch steps. Hunkering down before her, he took Rivers's hand in his own, studying the splinter.

Rivers gasped as, without pause, he drew her hand to his mouth, taking the exposed end of the splinter between his teeth tugging on it. "Ow!" Rivers exclaimed once more.

"Oh, quit your whinin', girl," Paxton scolded impatiently. He drew a small knife from his pocket.

"What are you doin'?" Rivers asked.

"I'm gonna cut your hand off, girl. What do ya think?" he grumbled.

"You don't have to . . ." she began, trying to draw her hand away from him.

But he held it firmly, placing the tip of the splinter between his thumb and the knife blade. He pulled the splinter out quickly and rubbed the sore area of Rivers's palm vigorously to ease the pain.

"It's takin' too long," he stated.

"What?" Rivers asked, puzzled. She wasn't at all certain what he meant.

"Weston and Jolee," he answered.

"It's only been a couple of weeks since . . ."

"Somethin's not right. Somethin's keepin' them from goin' ahead," he muttered, standing and offering his hand to Rivers. She took it, in return of his offered courtesy, and dusted off the back of her skirt.

"Somethin' like what?" she asked.

"Somethin' like you," he stated. For the first time in days, the intensity of his sapphire stare met hers.

"Me?" she asked, placing one hand to her bosom. Her heart began to throb with the intense pain stabbing her there as realization hit her. "You mean because I'm here . . . and she thinks I don't have anywhere to go? You think she's . . ."

"I think she wants somethin' to be goin' on between you and me, and that's why she won't give herself to him," he interrupted.

Paxton clenched his teeth tightly as he watched the expression of realization forming in Rivers's eyes. The same expression had once filled Ruby Dupree's—the expression of injury and heartbreak. He'd done it to her. He hadn't meant to, but it had happened. The difference being, if Rivers looked deep enough into his eyes, he knew she'd see the same emotion reflected there. He cursed himself for trapping the girl's heart. Yet he'd done it on purpose. The night by the pond found him weak and unable to resist her any longer. And here before him, the hurt all too apparent in her eyes, she stood—beautiful, desirable, perfect, and now hating him.

"Then I have to leave at once. Don't I?" Rivers whispered.

"No," Paxton corrected her. "She'd think me a lost cause then and never marry Weston."

Rivers looked away from him for a moment. He inhaled deeply and swallowed hard.

Paxton felt ill. Sickening heat seemed to tear through his body as he fought to resist pulling her into his arms. He was no good, a hardened, rough ol' bobcat with nothing to offer a warm, soft, sweet-tasting bunny like Rivers. He had to keep reminding himself she deserved better. He had to make sure he did not give in to his selfish desire to own her—she deserved better.

She looked back to him then, and it was nearly his undoing. Tears brimmed plentifully in her eyes, and he felt her pain piercing his own heart. He realized then his actions, or rather lack of action, had been breaking her for weeks. It was further proof, reassurance he did not deserve her.

Rivers thought she might die from the pain clenching her heart. As she looked at him, having already known this day would come, knowing she could never hope to own the heart of a man like Paxton Gray—as she looked at him, she asked, "Then what do you want me to do, Paxton? What do you want me to do? You tell me that because I'm here Jolee won't move further on with Weston. But then you tell me I can't go. What do you want me . . ."

"I want ya to help me convince her that I'll be fine without her here," he explained. "Let her think what she wants, and then when she finally accepts Weston . . . you can do whatever ya feel ya need to." He took a deep breath and looked out toward the fields nearby. "There was this girl, ya see. Years back. Jolee's worried I won't ever . . . that I . . ." he began.

"Ruby," Rivers stated and watched as he looked back to her quickly, surprise apparent on his face. "Jolee told me about your Ruby when I first came here."

"What did she tell you?" he asked, suddenly angry.

"That you were in love with a woman named Ruby. That's all I know. She left you, ran away or somethin', and you've never gotten over her," Rivers mumbled, struggling to keep the tears from spilling from her eyes.

Paxton inhaled deeply, and Rivers knew he was barely controlling his temper. Yet control it he did.

"I want ya to help me convince Jolee, Rivers. I want her to think . . . to think I've some interest in you—enough that she'll think if she marries Weston, you'll stay with me. She's wasted enough of her life takin' care of me." He chuckled and shook his head. "She loves me so much she can't see it makes me miserable to see her lettin' her life pass by because of it."

Rivers studied him as he gazed out over the fields. Oh, how attractive he was! The breeze caught the tousled locks of hair at his forehead and blew them back for a moment. She loved him! She would never love anyone like she loved Paxton Gray! She made a silent oath, promising herself she would never forget how wonderful he was, how handsome. He was compassionate, self-sacrificing. For all his selfish, crabby pretenses, he did not hide his true self very well. He had a heart, a feeling heart, though he would like everyone to think otherwise. Rivers knew his heart, knew him for his goodness as well as his physical beauty.

She'd always known Paxton Gray was only a dream to her—that a man such as he was would never give himself to an orphan girl who drifted from town to town by riding the rails. Yet she had so desperately wished that he would. But he wouldn't. She knew. *All good things must come to an end*, her father had always said. And so, end it must.

"I'll stay until we see Jolee married, then I'll be on my way," she told him. It was what he wanted to hear. "I promise."

Paxton looked back at her, nodding with appreciation, though he still wore a heavy frown.

"Let's start with a little outin'. Today," he said, "I told Weston to meet us here just before noon. Follow my lead, Rivers. That's all I ask. Follow my lead for a few days, and then ya can be on your way and rid of me."

♦ ♦ ♦ ♦ ♦

"Ya look pale, Rivers," Jolee said as she sat next to Rivers in the wagon later that morning. "Ya feelin' okay?"

Rivers forced a smile and nodded. "It's nice to get out, isn't it?" she said, trying to change the course of the conversation.

"Oh, yes. This'll be so fun. Just the four of us," Jolee sighed. "Paxton so rarely allows himself any relaxin' time lately." Jolee looked up, shading her eyes from the sun. "It's a little cloudy though. I don't know. We might get wet out here."

"We might," Rivers mumbled. She was certain her heart had tried to quit beating. She felt cold, lonely, empty. Glancing up at Paxton, however, she knew she would not simply fade away, for the hammering in her chest at the sight of him reminded her that the broken heart beats on.

• • •

Paxton halted the team and helped Rivers down from the wagon as Weston assisted Jolee. Just the simplest touch, the feel of her hand in his, caused Rivers's flesh to erupt into goose bumps. She wondered how she would endure life without such thrilling sensations to experience.

"Rivers has never seen the writin' on the rocks over here, Weston," Paxton remarked.

"It's purty interestin' if ya ask me, Rivers. How the Indians made pictures on the rocks and now we can look at 'em and try and figure what they were wantin' to say," Weston agreed, taking Jolee's hand and leading her toward a nearby rock formation.

"It looks like rain," Rivers commented.

"Naw, them clouds is just threatenin'. They won't do nothin'," Weston assured her.

"You look like a sick puppy, Rivers," Paxton whispered in her ear as they followed Weston and Jolee.

"Forgive me. I'm not comfortable lyin' to my friends," Rivers snapped.

"You're right. I guess Jolee wasn't your friend yet when ya showed up on the front porch askin' for work and lookin' like a boy," Paxton snapped in response.

"You're bein' cruel to me, Paxton," Rivers said, painful emotion rising within her.

"This here's my favorite," Weston called over

83

his shoulder, motioning for Paxton and Rivers to join him and Jolee. "See here," he explained. "This looks like a family to me. Ya see a man, a woman, then some children added in." He smiled flirtatiously at Jolee, and Rivers reached out to touch the markings with her own hand.

"It's lovely," she said. "I wonder what they made these with. You would think they would've worn away by now."

"I'm glad they haven't," Weston commented. "I've always found all this interestin'."

Rivers glanced up at Paxton to find his gaze firmly affixed on her. She uncomfortably cleared her throat and moved to a different impression on a nearby stone.

"That ol' tree is around here somewhere, ain't it, Paxton?" Weston asked a few moments later.

"What ol' tree?" Paxton grumbled. Rivers looked to him quickly, recognizing the irritated intonation of his voice.

"Don't play the dumb dog there, boy," Weston chuckled. "That ol' tree everyone carves their names in. Yeah! There it is. Yonder," he said, pointing to a huge and ancient-looking cotton-wood. "Come on, Jo . . . I'll show ya." Taking her hand in his, he led her in the direction of the tree, motioning for Paxton and Rivers to follow.

Paxton paused, seeming determined not to follow. "Come on, you old grumpy Gus," Rivers prodded, taking Paxton's hand and tugging on it. Paxton sighed, obviously irritated, but followed. Somehow, Rivers's curiosity was completely teased. She couldn't think why he would be so unwilling to look at an old tree with names carved in it. Still, if she was going to endure the kind of heartache their pretending was causing her, he could at least look at the old tree.

"See," Weston said, pointing to the trunk of the ancient tree. "Folks have been carvin' names in this tree since I was a little bit."

"Oh, look!" Jolee exclaimed. "There's Dan and Betty. Do you think that could be Dan and Betty Furman in town? Why, they're in their fifties!"

"Yep. That's them," Weston assured her. "Lookee here. Rebecca and Toby . . . that's the Millers in town. Jill and John Parker. There's all kinds that have carved here. Now, there's somethin' I seen here awhile back I need to ask Paxton about." Weston gestured for Paxton to follow him to the other side of the tree and Jolee and Rivers looked, too.

Rivers watched as a deep, rather worried frown wrinkled Paxton's brow as he looked at the tree. She followed his gaze and felt sorry for the child of Mother Nature when she saw the damage that had been done to it in one area.

"What do ya make of that, Pax?" Weston asked, pointing to an area brutally scarred with what looked like the lacerations made by a knife.

Rivers looked closely. Two names had been

carved in the tree where the vicious damage scarred it now. She swallowed hard, an odd sort of trepidation rising in her—Paxton and Ruby. The names carved in the tree beneath the more recent damage were "Paxton and Ruby." Indeed, someone had chopped at the lettering, leaving the deep and fairly fresh scars in the bark and wood beneath.

Paxton reached out and touched the area with his fingers, tracing the deep wounds of the tree. He shrugged his shoulders, still frowning. "Don't know. Someone just up to no good, I suppose," he mumbled.

"Maybe," Weston agreed. "But don't it strike ya as strange . . . them fresh cuts in this here tree . . . and me seein' Ruby in town yesterday?"

Rivers quickly looked to Paxton. His thoughts and feelings were not visible in the indifferent expression he now wore. In truth, his face suddenly seemed as lifeless as stone.

"Her family has moved back into town, Paxton. She's here with them for awhile. She's perty as ever and probably just as fickle," Weston said.

"She's a fine girl, Weston. She didn't do nothin' wrong," Paxton mumbled.

"Well, that may be true of Ruby . . . but her mama's with 'em, Paxton," Weston informed, lowering his voice.

Paxton quickly looked to Weston, who nodded.

Then he glanced at Rivers for a moment before studying the scarred tree again. "Maybe she's healin' then," Paxton suggested.

Weston raised his eyebrows disbelievingly. "I still wonder, Pax. This here does make me wonder."

Rivers felt her heart begin to constrict once more. Paxton still loved this Ruby. It was, however painful, very obvious. He defended her at every turn. Furthermore, the defacing of the tree seemed to bother him.

"Ruby perty much left ya at the altar, Paxton. How can you defend her like that?" Weston argued.

Rivers feared her stomach would become so upset from her painful emotions that she might be sick. She began to walk away from the others.

"Hush, Weston," she heard Jolee scold.

"It's time we had it out of him, Jo. If he's gonna ever get on with his life . . . it's time he put it behind him," Weston argued.

"It is behind me, Weston," Rivers heard Paxton tell his friend. Knowing he lied made her feel even more ill. She walked faster, but it wasn't long before she felt Paxton's powerful grip on her arm.

Turning to face him, she spoke before he could. "He's callin' your bluff, Paxton. He knows you . . ."

"Then I'll just call his, Rivers," he interrupted. "Let's walk awhile and give them a chance to cozy up a bit."

Still holding her arm, he linked it through his own and began walking with her. Being so near to him was an odd sort of intoxication. It sent Rivers's common sense, her rational thought spinning to the wind. She couldn't speak, afraid she might suddenly turn to him and confess her love, throw herself against him, beg for his kiss. And so she said nothing. They simply walked in silence, and for quite a distance.

"Ruby's mother was a bit . . . unstable," he said, unexpectedly breaking the awkward silence between them. "I figure it's her that tore up the tree like that. She was mighty angry when I . . ." He paused, seeming to reconsider what he was about to say, then continued, "Hey, we better head back. We've come quite a ways. I didn't realize how far we . . ."

His words were drowned out by a sudden clap of thunder. In the next instant, heavy rain poured down from the Heavens. Rivers looked to Paxton, who stood face turned upward, eyes closed, letting the moisture trickle down his face and neck.

"Let's get back. We'll get drenched!" Rivers said, wiping the rain from her eyes.

Paxton looked at her then. "Somethin' about sudden storms like this," he said. "They give ya two opportunities ya might not take at any other time."

"And what might those be?" she asked, brushing the wet hair from her forehead.

"You can cry your heart out and nobody's the wiser. That's one," he answered, reaching out and taking her hands in his own, as he pulled her closer to him. "And two, there ain't a better condition for sharin' a kiss." He drew her against the warmth of his powerful body, embracing her securely in his arms.

"Don't, Paxton. Please," Rivers begged as she felt several tears of heartache escape her eyes.

"Don't lose your nerve on me now, girl. Jolee and Weston are spyin' on us from just over there a ways," he whispered as he held her face firmly with one hand. "Close your eyes from the rain, Rivers," he whispered an instant before he took her mouth with his.

Rivers's body went limp in the strength of Paxton's arms and at the hot pressure of his mouth on hers. Her inner voice silently begged him to release her, to end the spell his kiss wove over her mind and body. Undone, Rivers gave into him entirely, letting herself revel in the feel of his hands on her waist and back—allowing her mouth, her senses to thoroughly savor the moist taste of his kiss. Yet the taste of her own tears intruded. Their salty flavor distracted her, reminded her he was kissing her simply for farce. Still, she savored the feel of being held by him, the warmth of his body against hers, the heat of his mouth instructing hers to join in some intimate dance. The taste of salt seemed to distract Paxton as well. He abruptly broke the seal of their lips, taking her face between his hands and intently studying her expression.

"It won't be long, girl. Then I'll release you. You'll be free to go," he comforted, misreading the cause of her tears.

"But I . . ." she stammered. How could she convey to him she didn't want to leave? That she never wanted to be without him? That she wanted to stay in his powerful arms forever, eternally savor his kisses?

"Now kiss me in the rain just once more, for Jolee's sake, Rivers," he mumbled as he released her face and let his hands slide around her waist, pulling her body flush with his own before again banding her in his arms.

She was breathless in his arms, found it difficult to breathe, for the rain was increasing and he held her so tightly. His final kiss was light and teasing. When he broke from her, he said, "Look," and tipped his head toward the direction from which they had come.

Rivers was torn between the pure delight burning within her at seeing Weston and Jolee some distance away embraced in an affectionate kiss, and the heartache she felt at having her own kiss end.

"Wooo whooo!" Paxton exclaimed unexpectedly. "I love a storm!" He reached back over his shoulders and took hold of his shirt, pulling it over his head and off his body. He stretched his arms out at his sides and turned his face upward again, letting the rain wash over his now bare torso. "You like me best when I'm just bathed, ain't that right, girl?" he asked as he motioned for Rivers to follow him as he started back toward the others.

The refreshing shower ended quickly, however. By the time they were all in the wagon, the sun was shining bright and high in the sky. This time returning home, Jolee sat with Weston as he drove the team, and Rivers found herself next to Paxton in the wagon bed.

Paxton stretched his arms along the sideboards of the wagon and breathed deeply. "Ain't nothin' like a quick shower to freshen up your mood, right?"

"I'm drenched," Rivers mumbled, a chill causing her to shiver slightly.

"Ya do look like a drowned kitten, now that ya mention it," Paxton chuckled as he studied her from head to toe.

"I think you owe me an explanation," Rivers blurted.

"About what?"

"About Ruby Dupree, and why she left you at the altar and why you still pine away after her," she said abruptly.

His amused smile faded then, his eyes narrowing as he looked at her. "I don't owe you no such thing, girl," he growled in a low voice.

"Yes. You do," Rivers argued. "I'm staying here at your request, remember?"

"You're stayin' here 'cause ya got nowhere else to go, remember?" he spat.

Rivers looked away from him and muttered, "You're right. Forgive me."

"I ain't told nobody the whole story, girl. Weston knows a tale or two of it, but not the whole thing. I went to her daddy about two weeks 'fore we were supposed to get married and told him I couldn't marry Ruby," Paxton confessed in barely a whisper.

Rivers looked at him quickly. "I wasn't in love with her. That's the meat of it. Then there was her mother . . ." he added, pausing.

"She's . . . she's mad?" Rivers asked. "Were you afraid that Ruby might inherit the insanity?"

Paxton shook his head. "Wouldn't have mattered to me if I had really been in love with her. I would've married her anyway. It was . . . well, her mother . . ." He sighed exasperated. "Dang it all, Rivers . . . I'm confessin' to ya here! Quit readin' things in. I didn't love the girl! I thought I did— thought I should. But I couldn't. Believe me, I tried. But when I told her daddy I was backin' out . . . well, they left that very night. They hired some folks in town to pack up their house and move their belongin's for them. Nobody heard a word from 'em . . . until now, I guess." He looked at her, and Rivers was shocked at the expression on his face. An expression of guilt and shame. "Ya see, I done her wrong."

"Marryin' her when you didn't love her would've been wrong, Paxton," Rivers assured him.

"Yeah? Well, you didn't see the look on her face when she walked in havin' overheard what I told her daddy," he grumbled.

But Rivers could all too well imagine what Ruby felt and how she had looked when she'd heard she had lost Paxton Gray. All too well did she hold an unspoken kinship with the woman.

She pressed her fingers to her lips, trying to smooth away the delightful sensation of his kiss lingering upon them. But it didn't help. She doubted anything ever would.

Paxton and Weston were unhitching the team when Jolee said to Rivers, "I want to check on Mary Belle, Rivers. Her udder was in sorry shape when I milked her this mornin'. Come with me, will ya?"

Rivers nodded and followed Jolee into the barn and toward the cow. "That was a nice piece of refreshment for us, wasn't it?" Jolee asked, kneeling down beside the animal.

"The storm? Oh yes," Rivers agreed.

Jolee giggled. "Well, that's not exactly what I meant, Rivers. But the storm was nice, too."

"Her udder still looks a bit irritated," Rivers answered, kindly patting the cow on the back.

"While we're out here," Jolee said, standing, "I'm lookin' for that little hatchet of Paxton's." She began rooting through some tools in a wooden box near the stall.

"Oh, I've seen it!" Rivers exclaimed as she walked toward an empty feed bin used for storage. "It's right down in here." Rivers groaned, however, as she noticed the silky spiderweb just inside the bin. "Oh! I can't stick my hand in there! Look at that web! It's huge!"

Rivers's one true fear was spiders. She'd tried and tried to overcome it all her life, but to no avail.

"I'll get it," Jolee giggled, coming to stand beside her.

"No. I've got to get over this," Rivers whispered, trying to force her hand into the bin.

"That's a widder web!" Jolee exclaimed.

"Black widow?" Rivers choked, quickly withdrawing her hand.

"Yeah. Looks like a big one! Look at the size of that web!" Jolee whispered. "Paxton would be very impressed. I really should get a jar and catch it for him."

Rivers wrinkled her nose and wondered why anyone would think to do such a thing. Then she watched in stunned horror as Jolee stuck her hand into the bin as if there were nothing at all to fear.

"Jo!" Rivers gasped quietly.

"Can't be scared of 'em, Rivers. Just leave 'em alone, and they won't hurt you."

Rivers's eyes locked on the hatchet's handle, and terror raced through her veins as Jolee pulled it from the darkness of the bin. A mere inch or less from where Jolee clutched the hatchet with one hand sat an enormous shining black spider.

Rivers screeched at the sight of the spider, startling Jolee, who jumped, dropping the hatchet. The spider, however, seemed to fly from the handle at the same moment and onto Jolee's dress.

"It's on you!" Rivers screamed.

"Where? Where? Get it off!" Jolee squealed, swatting madly at her bodice.

Rivers stood terrified as she watched the spider crawl up Jolee's sleeve and disappear under a strand of her hair hanging loosely over one shoulder.

"It's on my neck! I can feel it!" Jolee whispered.

The fear was plain on Jolee's face and finally broke the spell of panic paralyzing Rivers. Slowly, she moved the strand of hair. There, like an evil omen, was the spider. It was perfectly still, and sitting on Jolee's neck.

"What do I do?" Rivers asked in a desperate whisper.

"What in tarnation is goin' on in here? Sounds like a bunch of screamin' magpies," Paxton thundered as he and Weston burst into the barn.

"Paxton!" Rivers pleaded in a whisper, pointing to Jolee.

Paxton looked at the tears streaming down both female faces and went to his sister.

"Big ol' nasty one," he mumbled upon seeing the spider.

"Shoot!" Weston exclaimed in a whisper. "She's raised! She's gonna bite!"

Rivers watched in complete astonished fright as Paxton rapidly reached toward the threatening widow.

"Ow!" Jolee cried just before Paxton smashed the villainous, eight-legged creature between his thumb and forefinger. Rivers wrinkled her nose and clutched at her churning stomach at the gruesome sight of the spider's mossy green innards apparent on Paxton's fingers.

"Did it get ya?" Weston asked, his face stricken with concern.

"Yes!" Jolee cried as tears continued to stream down her face.

Rivers watched as Paxton quickly wiped the spider's remains on his trousers and bent down to scrape a block of cattle salt with his pocket knife. He spit onto the salt scrapings and roughly rubbed the stuff onto his sister's injured neck.

"Dang bad place to get bit," he muttered. "Venom will travel faster now. Let's get her to the house."

Rivers stood frozen with horror and could only stare as Weston gathered Jolee swiftly into his arms. Paxton brusquely pushed by Rivers as he strode out of the barn, motioning for Weston to follow.

As they entered the house, Rivers clamped her hand over her mouth and raced from the barn. When she'd reached the willow tree near the pond, she stopped and fell to her knees, sobbing. The shock of seeing the horrible spider was enough in itself. She was violently shaking and covered with an unpleasant sort of goose bumps. But to know it was her fault Jolee had been bitten was almost unendurable. As if in answer to her thoughts, at that very moment she heard the distant whistle of a train. She stood and listened intently. She wiped the moisture from her cheeks and took a deep breath.

"Don't even think about it now, girl!" Paxton growled as he grabbed hold of Rivers's arm, turning her to face him. "Jolee's gonna get mighty sick, and you need to be here to help her through it. It's a painful and sickenin' thing to endure . . . a widder bite. And I need you here to help her!"

"It's my fault," Rivers choked out.

"No, it ain't, and I don't have the time to stand here arguin' with ya about it. Jolee shoulda known better than to stick her hand in there!"

"I should've done it . . ."

"I'm goin' in to town to fetch some morphine from Doc Roberts. You go on back in the house and get her comfortable. Help Weston try to calm her down."

Then he added, "I will find you here when I get back." It was a command, not a question.

CHAPTER SIX

After being bitten, Jolee was painfully ill. The fever, nausea, and cramping caused by the spider's bite were continuous and miserable. Through it all, Rivers was guilt-ridden. If only she'd been able to overcome her fear of spiders and swat it from Jolee's sleeve. Rivers tormented herself time and again as she watched her friend endure the terrible consequences of the spider's venom. Though sweet Jolee continually reassured her, Rivers blamed herself.

Rivers sensed Paxton harbored his own feelings of guilt, though he had no fault. It seemed he talked with Rivers more easily. She assumed this was because he could not spend more time with his sister. Still, whatever the reason, Rivers couldn't help being delighted with his company. Any attention he gave her set her heart to fluttering, her skin to tingling, and left her breathless.

Weston was at Jolee's side every moment he could spare, their time together drawing them closer. It was obvious Weston felt helpless and angry. He silently endured his own pain as he watched Jolee endure hers.

At night, Rivers slept fitfully. She wished she had had the courage to leave before the incident occurred. She convinced herself Jolee would never have been in such a state were it not for Rivers's presence. She knew she should have left, hopped a train, and given Jolee and Paxton their lives to live without her interference. She hadn't, and now having to watch Jolee suffer was her punishment. Even after two long weeks, when Jolee was out of bed and nearly back to a daily routine, Rivers bathed in the anguish of guilt.

One morning, Jolee and Rivers stood at the sink working at the breakfast dishes. Weston came through the kitchen door and tipped his hat in greeting to the two women. Yet instead of speaking to Jolee as Rivers expected, he went directly to the table where Paxton sat reading a letter he'd received.

"I talked with Ruby Dupree today, Pax," Weston said in a lowered voice.

"Well, that's right nice of ya, Weston," Paxton grumbled.

"She asked about ya, Pax. How ya was, about your health, and if there was anybody particular puttin' the twinkle in your eye." Rivers listened intently, pretending to be fully engrossed in washing the dishes. She knew Jolee listened too, also feigning indifference.

"What did ya tell her, Weston?" Paxton asked. His voice revealed his annoyance. "Did ya tell her I got me my own little bit of a girl pinned up in the house against her will?" Rivers glanced over her shoulder. Paxton pointed at her. "Did ya let her know my affections are directed somewhere else now?" he shouted. Jolee turned to look at him.

"Paxton!" she scolded. "Weston is just trying to . . ."

"I know, I know," Paxton groaned. He quickly stood up, knocking his chair over in the process. "But that's the past. I don't want nothin' to do with any of them Duprees."

"Maybe it would be better for everyone concerned if you were to go over there and just greet them in a friendly manner, Paxton," Jolee suggested. "It will clear the air, and ya won't have such hard feelin's toward Ruby and her family."

Paxton shook his head and chuckled in disbelief. "Jo . . . I love ya. Ya know I do. Usually I wouldn't hide somethin' like this from ya—'cause ya don't know all that went on in this situation. Ya don't know, and since ya don't . . . ya can't . . ." He shook his head, stumbling over his words.

"Hey, I'm sorry, Pax," Weston apologized. "I didn't mean to upset ya. I just thought . . ."

"You're a good friend, Weston," Paxton said, patting Weston on the shoulder. "I guess it's time the wash was out for everyone to see."

Rivers watched as Paxton slowly ran a hand

through his dark hair, picked up his chair, and sat down once more.

"I told Rivers this already," he began. "And I suspect ya already guessed at part of it, Weston. Still, for your sake, Jo . . . ya oughta know that the night Ruby and her family left town . . . well, I'd gone to her daddy that day, and I told him I couldn't marry his daughter. I told him I didn't love her and I would only be doin' wrong by her if I married her."

"I do know that, Pax," Jolee said soothingly, sitting down in a chair next to her brother. "You told me."

Paxton shook his head. "There's more, Jolee. I didn't figure ladies oughta be hearin' of it, and I admit to ya, Weston . . . I was ashamed to tell ya, until now."

It unsettled Rivers as Paxton's gaze fell to her. He looked to her, not Jolee or Weston, as he continued. "Ruby came into the room when I was talkin' to her daddy. She'd heard everythin' I'd said to him, and she was cryin'. I hurt her. I should've 'fessed up long before I did. Anyway, she begged me and begged me . . . promisin' to make me a good wife. Promisin' to have as many babies as I wanted her to have . . . but I knew then, more than before even, that I couldn't marry the girl. Well, her daddy was the vision of controlled anger. He shook my hand and thanked me for comin' to him . . . for my honesty. He told me they held no hard feelin's and that I wasn't to worry about it. He said he admired my integrity."

Rivers swallowed with difficulty, thinking of Ruby and the heartache Paxton's confession must have caused her. Paxton picked up a fork still lying on the table and began fidgeting with it as he continued. "So . . . I left and went out to their barn where I'd left my horse. I'm gettin' ready to mount, and I hear someone come in behind me. I figure it's Ruby, but I turned around to see Mrs. Dupree standin' there for all the world to see in nothin' but her nightdress."

"You're kiddin' me?" Weston exclaimed.

"Tell tales I do not," Paxton confirmed. "She walks up to me and puts her arms around my waist all snugly and says, 'I knew you'd see through her to me, Paxton,' and I just stood there not knowin' what she was talkin' about." Paxton shifted uncomfortably in his chair and tossed the fork to the other side of the table. "She thought I called off my weddin' to her daughter 'cause I had my eye on her."

"That's ridiculous, Pax. Why would she think that?" Jolee asked.

" 'Cause she's completely mad," Weston answered, staring at Paxton intently. "Why didn't ya tell us this before?"

"There's more," Paxton said. Releasing a heavy sigh, he said, "So, I'm standin' there, not sure what to make of the lady, and she takes hold of my face all of a sudden and kisses me square on the mouth."

Jolee gasped, put a hand to her mouth and whispered, "Oh, Paxton!"

"I tried pushin' her away, and she starts goin' on and on about what a great lover I'll make for her . . . and I tell you this, Jo . . . she weren't talkin' about writin' secret letters and sparkin' on the front porch." Paxton paused, shaking his head. "I took her hands and held them tight in front of her and said, 'Mrs. Dupree, I think you better go on in the house.' But she kept grabbin' at me and tryin' to kiss me again. In a minute, Mr. Dupree walks in the barn, and I think I'm wolf bait, but he just says, 'Come along, Marianna. It's time you were in bed.' That's all he said. I tried to explain, but he just shook his head at me and again told her to come in. Everything happened so fast then. I guess she had the knife hidden in her nightdress pocket or somethin' 'cause the next thing I know she's screamin' at her husband at the top of her voice somethin' about how he's not gonna take her from her lover. How she's worked so hard to get me and all . . . and she runs at him, plantin' that knife square in his right shoulder."

"Dang!" Weston exclaimed softly, shaking his head. "Why didn't ya tell us all this mess, Pax?"

"I promised Mr. Dupree I wouldn't. I figured I owed their family that much after what I done," Paxton answered. "So ya see, Weston . . . I have less interest in that girl and her family than I do a swelled-up tick on a dead dog."

"I always wondered why ya were so quiet about what happened, Pax," Jolee said.

"Well, now ya know, sis. And now ya know why I kept it from you." Paxton looked at Rivers, quirked one eyebrow, and asked, "So, what do ya think of me now, girl?"

"I think you've borne a heavy burden for a long time that wasn't yours to bear," Rivers answered plainly. Paxton seemed startled at her reply, and Rivers turned her attention to the sink once again. Somehow she felt greatly relieved. She didn't know what she'd expected to hear, but it wasn't the fact Paxton really didn't love Ruby. She'd feared perhaps the opposite were true— that maybe he had only lied to her before.

"I've gotta get in to town today," Paxton said. Sighing and standing, he added, "Some fresh air oughta clear my head a bit. I'm sure you can entertain the womenfolk while I'm gone, can't ya, Weston?"

Weston and Jolee glanced to one another then back to Paxton. Weston finally stammered, "Well, shore. I suppose."

"Well, go on ahead," Jolee said, clearing her throat. It was obvious to Rivers that Paxton's story had greatly unsettled his sister. "Take Rivers with ya though. She needs a good airin' out." Jolee smiled at her friend. "It'll get her mind off me for a while. She still spends too much time worryin' about me. She blames herself for things about as easily as you do, Pax."

"Oh, no! I need to stay here with you, Jo," Rivers insisted.

"Weston can take me for a short ride this afternoon. You don't mind, do ya, Weston?" she asked.

"My pleasure, ma'am," Weston answered, grinning slyly at Jolee.

"Why don't you two just say ya wanna get off in the bushes and spark awhile, Jo?" Paxton grumbled.

"Okay. I just wanna get off in the bushes and spark with my beau, Paxton. So you two be on your way. Go to town and get some fresh air, Rivers," Jolee giggled, winking at Weston, who winked back.

Paxton stretched and ran his fingers through his hair again. "Well, come on, girl," he said to Rivers. "Let's get goin'. Maybe I'll play ya a tune on the way," he added.

"I'm not goin'. I'll just stay here and darn some socks," Rivers sighed.

"Nope," Paxton yawned. "Jo wants us gone so she can love all over Weston, so we're goin'. I think we owe her that much." Taking Rivers's arm, he pulled her out of her chair and to her feet.

"Pick up some brown sugar, Rivers. We're runnin' low," Jolee called after them.

Rivers waved to a smiling Jolee as Paxton pulled her out the door. She smiled to herself, happy Jolee was well enough to spend time with Weston again.

Over the past few days, Jolee had confided in Rivers about her developing relationship with Weston. Rivers was happy for her. Jolee's smile, the twinkle in her eyes was radiant whenever she spoke of Weston. Still, she also felt somewhat fearful about Jolee finding out Paxton had kissed her—as if Jolee might think less of her for allowing herself to be so beguiled by Paxton's charms. Yet what woman could resist him? Even the mad Mrs. Dupree had been captivated by his allure.

Yet, as Rivers watched Paxton hitch the team, she hoped Jolee would taste of Weston's kiss again. Her own heart leapt with excitement in anticipation for her dear friend.

"What're ya grinnin' about?" Paxton asked as he helped Rivers onto the buckboard.

"Nothin'," she said.

Paxton clicked his tongue, and the team lurched forward. "She's lookin' better," he commented.

"Yes. At last," Rivers sighed, feeling the familiar pangs of guilt in her bosom.

"It wasn't your fault," Paxton said. She didn't respond. "Jolee should've known better. I've been bit a couple a times myself, and I've warned her over and over again. It ain't a fun thing to go through. But it sure ain't the worst."

Rivers didn't want to discuss Jolee's misery any longer, so without thinking, she blurted out the first question that came to mind.

"Why haven't you ever courted anybody since Ruby, Paxton?" Immediately, she regretted her thoughtless question. She looked over at the man driving the team, but there seemed to be no expression of any emotion on his face.

"That's a heck of a question to be comin' from you," he growled finally. "Bein' you won't let any of the men 'round here come courtin' you."

"I'm sorry. It's none of my business," Rivers replied, attempting to smooth things over.

"Ruby's mother scared me off," he said, answering her question all the same. "Why is it you won't give a nod to any of the fellers I know?" he asked.

"I . . . I . . . they don't interest me," Rivers stammered.

"Well, there ya have it. That's my own answer, too."

"But it's different with you. You're so . . . I mean, you know people around these parts. The women around here fawn over you somethin' awful! It seems to me that . . ."

"It seems to me that this ain't none of your concern, Rivers. Don't you be sidin' up with my sister in tryin' to marry me off to some silly . . ."

"I'm not! I was just curious as to why you . . . don't seem interested in . . ."

"I never said I wasn't interested in women, if that's what you're gettin' at. I'm all man, through and through, if that's what you're worried about," he chuckled.

"I wasn't doubtin' that," Rivers sighed.

"Dang right! You, of all people, should have reason enough not to doubt me there," he muttered, a sly grin spreading across his handsome face.

"It is impossible to hold a civil conversation with you, Paxton Gray!" Rivers exclaimed as she blushed. She couldn't believe he'd referred to their kisses. She was delighted by his referring to it, but shy in the same moment.

"You ever take it to mind maybe that's the way I want it?" he said, his smile fading.

Rivers tried to change the course of the conversation. "My, my. It is dry out here today. The very air feels . . . dry."

Paxton looked up at the sky beginning to cloud a bit. "Yep."

Rivers sighed again. He muddled her thoughts so when he was this near to her. She felt like confessing, *I love you, Paxton! I can love you like Ruby never could!* But she knew it would be futile. He would never see her as anything but a friend of Jolee's—a girl who had hopped off a train from somewhere. He hadn't wanted

Ruby Dupree. Why ever would he want her?

"You drive 'em," Paxton said abruptly, handing her the lines to the team. Taking his harmonica from his pocket, he tapped it in the palm of his hand. "What'll it be?" he asked her.

Rivers loved when he played. Often she would hear him out in the barn at night playing mournful tunes. But it was rare he played in front of anyone, even Jolee.

He played for some time then, tunes Rivers knew and tunes she didn't recognize. It was peaceful and yet—somehow haunting. Still, it relaxed her, made her appreciate the beauty of the day even more.

CHAPTER SEVEN

Once in town, Paxton left Rivers in the general store and went on toward the blacksmith. Rivers purchased the brown sugar Jolee had requested and then sat down on a bench on the front porch of the general store to wait for Paxton's return. She looked up, watching the clouds changing shape and color. It was a beautiful day—warm, bright, filled with sunshine.

Suddenly, she sensed someone stood near to her. Turning, Rivers saw an uncommonly attractive young woman standing over her. The woman stared at her, glared at her somewhat rudely.

"Are you the girl who's staying with the Grays?" the young woman asked.

Rivers's heart began to pound furiously as she knew at once who the woman was. "Yes," she gasped. "I'm Rivers Brighton." She offered her hand to the young woman, who took it and gently squeezed it in greeting.

"I'm Ruby Dupree. My family just returned to town," the girl explained. Rivers noted the perfect spun-straw sunshine hue of the woman's hair—the blue of her eyes so closely colored with Paxton's. "How are Paxton and Jolee?" Ruby inquired.

"Fine. Jolee's been ill, but she's recovered fully, I believe," Rivers answered.

"And . . . and Pax?"

"He's fine. Working hard as always."

"Yes, of course. He would be." Ruby's attention seemed to be captured by something behind and beyond Rivers. "Here he is now!" she exclaimed, waving frantically.

Rivers turned and watched Paxton approach.

"Paxton!" Ruby greeted as she hugged him tightly for a moment. "My, don't you look as handsome as ever?" She almost sighed the remark. Rivers could see the life Paxton's presence put into the blue of Ruby's eyes. Her own heart seemed to sink to the pit of her stomach.

"If you'll excuse me . . . I'll let you two visit for a moment," Rivers said, rising from her seat on the bench. She forced a smile and turned to leave. Paxton's firm grip on the back of her neck stopped her.

"We've got to be gettin' home to Jolee," he said to Rivers. Then he smiled at Ruby and said, "It's nice to see ya, Ruby. Tell your daddy I said 'hello.' "

Ruby nodded and smiled. Paxton tipped his hat to her as he directed Rivers toward the wagon, his hand still at the back of her neck.

"You can quit directing me by the scruff of the neck like a bad puppy, Paxton," Rivers snapped once they reached the wagon. She pushed his hand from her neck and climbed into the wagon unassisted.

"What's got your tail in a fuzz, girl?" he asked. Then he chuckled and added, "If I didn't know better, I'd think you were jealous."

"Well, you do know better," Rivers assured him. "Now, let's get home. I'm worried about Jolee."

"I hope Weston don't drag her off too far. She'll be a might weak for awhile yet," Paxton thought out loud.

"I'm sure he won't. A nice long ride with him will do her a world of good," Rivers said. "Miss Dupree is very beautiful," she added. She grimaced, irritated by the snap in her voice.

"She's a purty enough girl," Paxton admitted. "I feel bad for her, saddled with a mother like that."

Rivers's rising anger softened at the memory of Paxton's experience. He was a good man. He'd done the right thing on both counts, and she admired him for it. Still, she resented the fact he had been so closely involved with another girl, even if it was in the past.

"This sudden breeze is nice," she said. "So refreshing."

Paxton looked up into the sky. The clouds hung in low, green-gray clusters.

"I don't like the look of them clouds," he muttered.

"I think they're nice. I don't think I've ever seen anything like them before," Rivers said, inhaling deeply. "Smells like rain maybe."

Paxton looked up at the ominous clouds once again. "I think we better be gettin' on home."

Rivers began to feel uneasy at the speed with which Paxton was driving the team toward home. There was a deep, worried frown across his face, and he'd said very little since leaving town.

"What is it?" Rivers asked finally.

"Those clouds," he stated.

"What about them?"

"They're strange. I heard tell of them before. Come right along with twisters."

"Twisters?" Rivers asked. "You mean tornadoes?" she gasped.

"That's what I'm afraid of. See the way they're movin'. I don't like the look of it. And the wind is pickin' up too."

The wind had indeed picked up. The sweet breeze of a few minutes before was almost an unpleasant, full-blown wind now.

"Paxton?" Rivers said nervously.

"It's all right. We'll get home and let the stock loose, just in case."

"In case?"

"Well, it don't look like the clouds stop just here. I reckon this storm's headin' for our place as well."

Rivers was silent the rest of the way home. By the time they reached the farm, the wind was so strong it was almost impossible to stand straight.

Anxiety had driven her jealousy from her. The weather was turning evil.

Paxton lifted Rivers down from the wagon. "Make sure Jo's not in the house. Then you get your little fanny down in the root cellar. You hear me?" he hollered over the rushing air.

Rivers could hardly hear him above the roaring wind, but she nodded. She watched as he frantically unhitched the team and slapped one of the horses on the flank. Then she headed for the house.

"Jolee! Jolee, are you in here?" she called. There came no answer, so she checked all the rooms. Maybe she and Weston had sheltered somewhere else.

As quickly as she could, Rivers worked her way down the front steps and toward the cellar. The wind was a torrent of fury, sending leaves, twigs, and other debris pelting her face and body. She heard a horrible crackling sound and turned to see a nearby fence post break in two. It made a morbid noise as it flew up in the air, ripping the barbed wire off the post next to it.

Rivers screamed and ducked as the post and wire hurled through the dirt toward her! She felt herself hit the ground hard as the wire caught in the skirt of her dress. Frantically, she tried to stand up, but the gusty winds kept her down, and she became entangled even more severely in the wire. It cinched about her calves, the barbs biting through her stockings and into her flesh.

An ear-shattering roaring commenced. Rivers looked up, horrified at the sight of the forming funnel arching down from the sky into the pasture. The barbs of the wire rooted in her skirt and petticoats were tearing at the flesh of her legs. Reaching down, she struggled with the wire, trying to pull herself free.

"Strip your dress off!" came Paxton's shouting. A moment later, he was there, kneeling down in front of her and ripping open the bodice of her dress. "Get out of it! Shoes, too! Now!" he repeated.

Rivers quickly peeled her arms out of her dress as Paxton pulled a knife from his boot and cut the laces of her shoes. Tossing her shoes aside, Paxton tugged at the fabric of the skirt and petticoats until, at last, he was able to slip them down and over her feet.

Paxton pulled Rivers to her feet and pushed her ahead of him. "Run! Get in the cellar!" he shouted.

The dirt and debris blowing madly about made it almost impossible to see. At last, Rivers dropped to the ground and fumbled with the latch to the cellar door. She could hear a thunderous roar. She turned to see the devastating tornado touching down in the north pasture. The sound was deafening! It hurt her ears! But there was no time to pause and cover them.

Suddenly, she was shoved from behind and went tumbling down into the cellar. Then there was only the roaring of angry tempestuous wind above ground and complete darkness below.

Rivers breathed a sigh when at last she saw the flicker of a lantern as Paxton lit it. He came forward and knelt before her. He said something, but the roaring was so loud she couldn't hear him.

The horrible sound grew louder and louder, accompanied by the pounding vibrations of objects crashing about outside. Rivers put her hands to her ears and tried to block it all out. It was terrible! Never in her life had she experienced such a deep, foreboding anxiety as she did now. Her ears felt as if they might swell and burst from the racket. She could taste dirt in her mouth, and her legs throbbed with the ache of the barb wounds. The darkness of the enclosed cellar seemed like a tomb, and she felt fear being replaced by panic and heightening within her.

Rivers watched as Paxton sat down next to her on the cold, hard earth. His chest, neck, and face were bleeding. As she looked close, she realized a piece of barbed wire must have struck him, for the wounds appeared to be about three to four inches apart. Reaching up she touched his face. He winced and pushed her hand away.

Setting the lantern on the ground in front of him, Paxton rested his arms on his knees, enfolding the powerful limbs and letting his head rest on them.

Deafening, wrenching, cracking, popping, snapping noises commenced. Rivers shivered and waited as Paxton looked up and strained his ears.

He looked to Rivers and, though she heard no sound, she read his lips as he said, "The barn."

The roaring seemed to lessen a little, and Rivers looked up as if she might be able to see something through the wooden doors above them. There was little light sifting through the cracks between the wooden planks.

She looked back at Paxton and found him blankly staring at her. She thought how handsome he was, his face smudged with blood and dirt, his hair windblown. Then, as his eyes moved the length of her and back, she was awash with humiliation, as she realized she sat clad solely in her camisole, corset, and pantalets. She crossed her arms over her bosom, hugging herself and hoping his attention would soon be diverted. But by what?

Suddenly, the wind seemed to lose some of its strength. Although it still roared, sounding thunderous and violent, Rivers thought the tornado must be moving on—on to spread further fear and destruction.

They sat in silence for a few minutes more. Then Paxton spoke. "It's a bit breezy out this afternoon, ain't it?"

Rivers began to laugh and cry at the same time, fatigue and emotional distress weakening and confusing her emotions.

Instantaneously, the wind picked up again. Paxton stood, opening the cellar door just a crack. Slamming it shut, he shouted, "It's another one!" just before the wind resumed its ear-splitting roar.

Rivers doubled over and tried to block out the sound. She covered her ears, sobbing bitterly. She felt Paxton's hands on her shoulders and looked up at him as he hunkered down before her.

"It will pass," he mouthed to her. Rivers shook her head. The noise, the fear was driving her mad. She felt the need to scream—scream until her lungs burst!

Paxton took her face in his powerful hands, forcing her to look at him.

"We'll be fine," his lips said, and suddenly she felt lost in the blue of his eyes. She trusted him. If Paxton Gray said they would be all right, then she knew they would be. In those moments, gazing into the handsome strength of his face, Rivers knew he would keep her safe—Paxton would prevent harm from finding them there in the cellar.

Tenderly, Paxton held Rivers's lovely, frightened face in his hands. Tears streaked her dust-covered cheeks. He held his breath a moment then, astonished as he saw the fear in her eyes changed to trust. In those moments, Rivers placed her life in his hands, and somehow it both pleased and frightened him.

He released her, sitting down and leaning back against the earthen wall of the cellar. Propping his arms on his knees, he motioned for her to come and sit with him. She hesitated for only a moment and then, much to his surprise, actually nestled herself safely against him. She leaned her back against his chest, astounding him next by taking his hands and wrapping herself snugly in his arms.

Paxton let his chin rest on the top of her head, and, for all the swirling dust, he could still smell the sweet scent of her hair. To have her there in his arms, against his body . . . it was pure pleasure. Small and slight she may be, but he knew she was strong and capable as well. Still, she needed his comfort. He knew she needed him, only him. And, for those next few moments, he decided to let her need him.

Rivers felt secure in Paxton's arms. He was warm and strong. His breath in her hair sent goose bumps erupting along her arms and legs. The feel of his powerful hands on her arms both calmed and excited her. She felt she could breathe easier, yet was more breathless than before.

Outside, the wind began to diminish once again. Yet in its place there was a new sound—the sound of heavy rain hitting the earth and cellar door. Quickly, however, the wind became a gentle breeze, and the rain fell softly.

"Is it over?" Rivers asked quietly. Her own voice sounded strange to her ears, which were still ringing with the wicked roar of the wind.

"Probably," Paxton answered. "But we'll sit here awhile, just in case."

Rivers couldn't have asked for anything more blissful than to sit in Paxton's arms forever. But she turned to look at him, and he released her, though he made no move to stand.

"Your face!" she exclaimed, upon seeing the wounds there once more.

He reached up and touched one of the wounds, looking at the blood it left on his fingers. "I think a piece of that barbed wire flew up at me when we were gettin' ya untangled."

Rivers reached up and caressed his cheek, being careful of the wounds. "I'm sorry, Paxton," she said.

Paxton shifted uncomfortably. Much more of this and he'd break. After all, there she sat, right up against him. And her lack of proper clothing wasn't helping matters! He smiled and thought to himself how cute she looked in just her under things.

"What?" Rivers asked as the smile spread across Paxton's face.

"Nothin'," he answered.

Suddenly, Rivers was overwhelmingly self-conscious. "Tell me! What?" she demanded.

"Well, it's just that . . . well . . . ya look so danged cute in just your drawers," he chuckled.

Rivers looked down at herself. He thought she was "cute"? There she sat in attire to put most men out of their minds, and he thought she was cute!

"Well . . . I guess that's meant as a compliment," she muttered, as a frown wrinkled her brow.

"Of course it was. What did ya want me to say?" Paxton teased. "Now, sit back and rest. We'll go out in a while."

Rivers frowned as she leaned back against him once more. Still a bit miffed at his remark about her being cute, she almost didn't notice at first when he moved her hair to one side. She noticed first his hand brush lightly against her neck. Then he put his chin to her temple and pushed gently, directing her head to tip to one side.

"What are you doing?" she whispered.

"Don't ask stupid questions, Rivers," he answered, just before she felt his mouth on the sensitive flesh of her neck.

Rivers flinched at his kiss as the rushing ripple of goose bumps raced over her entire body—a fact that Paxton apparently did not miss, for he caressed her arm, chuckling quietly. He kissed her neck again and then turned her head toward his and kissed her cheek. The warmth of his breath on her neck and ear, the caress of his lips to her cheek were purely rapturous sensations. He toyed with her for long moments, kissing her cheek, letting his breath warm the flesh of her neck and shoulder. It was almost torturous! She wanted to feel his mouth against her own, taste the warm moisture of his kiss! She was breathless, struggling to appear calm and unruffled. It was nearly impossible to remain still!

Finally, he turned her body, cradling her head and shoulders in one arm and gazing somewhat drowsily down at her. He let his fingers lightly caress her neck, traveling down toward her shoulder. For a moment he toyed with the strap of her camisole, pushing it from her shoulder. Rivers shuddered with delight as the strap slipped further down her arm. Caressing the bareness of her arm with one powerful hand, he paused a moment before placing a moist, lingering kiss on her shoulder. He kissed her there again, letting his fingertips caress her shoulder then and sending Rivers's body into another fit of goose bumps

"You're . . . you're just trying to get my mind off of the storm," Rivers stammered in a whisper.

"Darlin', the storm's just startin' down here," Paxton mumbled.

And then, at last, he let his mouth discover hers in a driven, succulent kiss. He held her tightly, cradled against him, as his free hand traveled over the soft smoothness of her neck, shoulders, and arms. His touch was igniting to her senses! Paxton had kissed her before. He'd touched and held her before. But never in such a soft, intimate manner as this. The sensation of his strong, calloused hands on her skin was magnificent! Oddly, the thought briefly passed through her mind that he was to be trusted—but for the scandalous truth of their circumstances, Paxton Gray was a gentleman and would not let his hands stray to any part of her being inappropriate.

Rivers's hand had been resting gently against Paxton's chest, but now instinctively slipped beneath his shirt, torn open by the violent wind. His skin was heated and caused the tips of Rivers's fingers to tingle with delight in the feel of him.

Their kisses were as the first hint of a storm, refreshing, calming, with the promise of more. And then, just as the storm had done, their passion grew, mounting into a powerful force. Rivers let her hand slide upward and around to the back of Paxton's neck. Paxton pulled her against his own body, and she thought he might crush her, so tightly did he hold her. She basked in the sensation racing through her entire being, in the bliss of touching him in such a familiar manner.

It further enchanted her when she felt him shiver, his own body suddenly consumed with goose bumps, as her hand traveled caressingly over his strong, impressive chest once more. He tightened his embrace, seeming unable to quench some raging crave, for his kisses were near to unmerciful.

Suddenly, doubt and fear, the devil's finest tools, infected Rivers's mind. It couldn't be happening! She couldn't be wrapped in Paxton Gray's arms, his mouth working a bewitching spell of affection and desire over her! It couldn't be real! It was simply the circumstances, the state of her undress finding him so easy with her.

Rivers abruptly broke the seal of their kiss, turning her face from his.

"You're . . . you're only teasing me again. Jolee isn't here to witness this, Paxton. And I'm not something for you to play with," she cried.

"I'm not teasin' ya this time, Rivers. And I'm well aware Jolee ain't here to be watchin'," Paxton whispered as he took her chin in hand, turning her face back to his. He stroked her dusty, tear-streaked cheek with his thumb and smiled. "When this storm is over, I'll be my charmin', heartless self again. You can go back to thinkin' I'm an ol' grouch, who don't care about nobody. But for right now . . . down here in the cellar, where no one but you can see me, I'll tell you a secret. You know that Ruby Dupree girl you met today and know so much about?"

Rivers nodded and shivered as his thumb traveled over her tender lips.

"Well, ain't a woman in this whole world that ever got me wrapped around her finger like you do—even her. I oughta tan your backside for that, Rivers Brighton," he whispered.

Then she watched in blissful anticipation as Paxton's head descended toward her own again. His lips toyed with hers this time, barely brushing hers teasingly for a moment, then retreating only to tempt her over and over. She held her breath as he placed a whiskery cheek to her soft one, pausing in his taunting of her. Her hands gripped his shoulder tightly as she felt the slightest touch of his tongue on her throat before his mouth began placing teasing kisses there. When, at last, he turned his attention anew to her mouth, his kiss was wet, driven, fiery, forceful, and filled with a scarcely restrained passion. Paxton's kiss caused a tempestuous trembling to torment Rivers's soul—rendering her mind uncertain she could continue to prevent her very being from flying apart, the pieces joining the heavens as new and resplendent stars there.

He was so warm, powerful, dominant! She never wanted to leave the cellar! Oh, couldn't the heavens just leave her there? Couldn't she bathe in those moments forever?

All too soon, however, the dream-borne figure of a man ended their kissing, adeptly maneuvering Rivers's body until her back lay against his chest once more. Paxton folded his arms around her and let his legs relax, stretched out on the ground.

"It must be dark by now," he said quietly. "We'll wait a while longer. I ain't in a hurry to see the mess up there."

Rivers let her head fall back against Paxton's massive chest. The storm and the passionate exchange with Paxton seemed suddenly overwhelming. Rivers was exhausted and soon fell into a deep, contented slumber—safe in the powerful arms of Paxton Gray—safe in the arms of the man she loved.

CHAPTER EIGHT

"Are they in there?"

Rivers forced her heavy eyelids to open. The voices had pulled her from a heavy sleep. She looked up just as the doors above her were unlatched and light streamed into the cellar. There, peering down into the darkness, were Weston and Jolee.

"Oh! My goodness!" Jolee exclaimed.

"You've been down there all night?" Weston asked.

Paxton pushed Rivers forward and stood up, stretching and groaning.

"Dang, my rear-end is numb as a dead man's," he grumbled.

Rivers struggled to her feet as well, shielding her eyes from the bright morning sun.

"You two look purty beat up. But wait 'til ya see what's gone on up here," Weston sighed, his discouragement all too obvious.

Paxton bolted up the stairs and through the cellar door as Jolee reached down and helped Rivers climb up. The sight that met them was horrifying. Rivers gasped at what her eyes beheld—debris consisting of wood, tree limbs, buckets, broken glass, wire, splintered fence posts, and other rubble littered the ground everywhere.

"Looks like you're gonna be havin' a barn raisin' 'round here, friend," Weston said.

"The barn," Paxton muttered, his voice void of discernible emotion.

Rivers turned and followed his gaze in the direction of the barn. "It's completely gone," she whispered.

All that remained of the once enormous and indestructible-looking barn was a pile of rubble.

"The windows blew out of the house, too, Pax," Jolee added. They all turned and stared at the house. The broken glass was lying all over the ground. Not one window was left intact.

"Have ya been inside yet?" Paxton asked.

"Yeah. Seems to have weathered purty well. Just some things blown around," Weston answered.

Rivers took several steps toward it but stopped cold when she felt a sharp, cutting pain in her foot.

"Ya lost your shoes, too?" Jolee asked as Rivers exclaimed in unexpected pain.

Paxton strode over to where she stood pulling the slivers of glass out of one stocking foot.

"She got wrapped up in some barbed wire . . . had to strip her nearly to the skin to get her free," he explained as he easily lifted her into his arms.

Rivers was silent as Paxton carried her into the house, knowing this would, indeed, be the last time he held her in his capable arms. The others followed in silence. Once inside, he set her down gently on the sofa and took a deep breath as he looked around.

"Well, the house seems fine." Running his fingers through his hair, he added, "At least we're all safe and sound." Then Paxton looked from Weston to Jolee and back. "Where did the two of you hold up? When we didn't find ya here . . . we didn't have time to look anywhere else."

"We ended up out at McGinness Point. Ya know that old cave out there in them big rocks? We just pulled the horses on in with us and waited it out," Weston said.

Paxton nodded and Jolee exclaimed, "Rivers! Your legs! And your face, Paxton! You both need a good washin' and some bandages."

"Don't she look cute in her drawers, Jo?" Paxton chuckled.

"For cryin' in the bucket, Paxton! She's bruised up, cut all over . . . quit your teasin'," Jolee scolded.

"You do look awful cute in your drawers, Miss Brighton," Paxton said, smiling and winking at Rivers. "Gives a man quite an appetite."

"Get out, Paxton!" Jolee ordered. "You go down and wash up at the pond before you send Rivers to faintin' away at your scandalous remarks!"

"I'm goin'," Paxton chuckled.

Rivers blushed as Paxton winked at her once more before leaving.

"I swear," Jolee sighed. "That man! The way

he's goin' on you're probably lucky ya didn't find your virtue in danger . . . trapped down there with him all night. What a nightmare that must've been."

But Rivers couldn't help but smile. Nightmare? Far from it! It had been more like a dream come true, and Rivers smiled as goose bumps suddenly covered her arms at the memory of Paxton's attentions in the cellar.

"You must be cold, Rivers!" Jolee said upon noticing the goose bumps on Rivers's skin. "Would ya be so kind as to help me fill a tub for Rivers, Weston?"

"Of course, Jolee," Weston said, winking at Rivers. "But I'm sure Paxton didn't let Rivers stay too cold down there in that cellar. Ain't that right, Rivers?"

Rivers blushed once more as Weston knowingly winked at her.

"Oh, don't be ridiculous, Weston," Jolee said, shaking her head. "It's freezin' down in that cellar."

"I'm sure it is," Weston chuckled. "You'll have to show me some time, Jolee."

Rivers smiled then, amused by Weston's teasing and Jolee's innocence. Again, her arms tingled with goose bumps, and she knew it would take a very warm, very long bath indeed to dispel them.

♦ ♦ ♦ ♦ ♦

"We wanna thank ya all for comin' out today. I know a lot of you folks had damage from the storm, and we want ya to know we're more than willin' to help out any way we can," Jolee shouted to the crowd of people gathered outside in front of the house.

Rivers smiled as her eyes met Paxton's and he winked at her. He'd begun flirting with her mercilessly since the storm. She had fully expected he would be true to his word about reverting to his regular glum self, but he hadn't. Hope burned bright in Rivers every moment of every day. Maybe she could win him away from his guilt about Ruby and his unpleasant remembrance of her mother.

Rivers watched as the men who had come to help raise the barn began their task. It was very interesting to watch a barn begin from nothing but a foundation of sorts and rise to the skeleton it became some hours later.

"Hey, girl," Paxton greeted, breathless from exertion. Striding to meet her and smiling, he wiped the sweat from his forehead with his shirt sleeve. "What do ya think? Looks good so far, don't it?" he asked.

"It's gonna to be bigger than the first one," she answered, brightly smiling up at him.

"Yep. I figure, might as well do it right, ya know?"

Rivers looked up into Paxton's rugged face and couldn't keep a sigh from escaping her lungs.

Paxton lowered his voice and said, "Whew! I'll

tell ya what! Work like that in heat like this . . . sure gives a man a mighty big appetite!"

"Oh, I'll fetch you a plate from the house and . . ." she began, but her words were cut short as he took hold of her arm and led her to the far side of the house.

"What are you doin'?" she asked, puzzled. Her heart pounded furiously.

Pushing her back against the outer wall of the house, his mouth exhausted hers with an unexpected, feverishly hot, magnificently forceful kiss, which left her weak, breathless, and light-headed.

"Ah!" he sighed. "That's better. Nothin' like your cherry-sweet kiss to satisfy a man's hunger!"

"What?" she exclaimed, looking around quickly to see if anyone had witnessed the exchange. And it had, indeed, been an exchange, for she had willingly supplied the confectionary nourishment he spoke of.

Paxton bent his head to repeat the refreshment, but a moment before joining his lips to hers, he stopped. Rivers was puzzled as an odd expression swept over his face. He straightened and looked past her toward the barn.

Rivers's attention followed the direction of his stare. A wagon with several passengers was arriving. Paxton stood frozen as if etched in granite. His eyes narrowed and the frown, absent from his brow for several weeks, returned.

"Paxton?" Rivers whispered.

As the wagon approached, she recognized Ruby and breathed, "Ruby."

"The whole dang family," Paxton growled.

Rivers watched as a beautiful, fair-haired woman the exact elder image of Ruby approached Jolee. Jolee seemed to greet the woman politely, but without her usual exuberance. Rivers felt her blood run cold. She stood paralyzed with anxiety as the woman began walking to where she and Paxton stood, having shared a passionate trade only moments before. Glancing up at Paxton, Rivers saw his face was still as hard and as cold as any stone figure.

"Paxton! Darling!" the woman called as she gracefully rushed toward him. Reaching him, she threw her arms around his neck and clung to him without any obvious concern for propriety. "Oh, Paxton! Dear boy! How wonderful to see you again!" the woman cried.

"Mrs. Dupree," Paxton greeted, not returning the embrace.

Mrs. Dupree released the man and turned. Somewhat sneering and smiling at the same time, she studied Rivers. Her nose wrinkled as if she had suddenly been nauseated by some bitter taste in her mouth.

"You must be Jolee's little friend I've heard about," she greeted, extending one daintily gloved hand toward Rivers. Rivers took the woman's hand but said nothing. "I suppose Paxton has told you all about how absolutely wicked he was to our daughter," the woman whispered, as if telling a terrible secret.

"No," Rivers managed to say. She looked up at Paxton, who stood staring down at Mrs. Dupree in complete astonishment as if he still could not grasp the actuality of her presence before him.

Mrs. Dupree looked from Paxton to Rivers and back. Then, placing a hand dramatically to her bosom, she whispered, "Have I interrupted a little . . . moment here, Paxton dear?"

"It wasn't a *little* moment, Mrs. Dupree," Paxton answered.

Mrs. Dupree smiled understandingly and winked at Rivers. "You be careful with this boy, dear. He's a heartbreaker that one. By the way, do call me Marianna."

Then, instantly, her expression changed. Her teasing, friendly smile was completely obliterated—replaced with a countenance akin to repulsion as she turned and walked away.

"Nutty as an acorn tree," Paxton mumbled.

"She's still wantin' you," Rivers plainly stated.

Paxton looked at Rivers, his eyebrows raised in surprise. "Wantin' me?" he questioned. "What makes you think you know when a woman's wantin' a man?"

"It's painfully obvious, Paxton. Your mule would know it," Rivers said. She didn't like the very feel of the air about her now that Mrs. Marianna Dupree had been breathing it. It felt polluted, poisoned somehow.

Paxton shook his head. "That woman don't want me, girl. I'm surprised she even remembers who I am, as batty as she is."

Rivers took Paxton's face firmly between her hands and spoke directly to him. "You be careful. She's not right in the head. She stabbed her own husband for cryin' out loud, Paxton!" she warned in a whisper.

"Why, Rivers," Paxton teased, "I believe you're truly concerned for me."

Rivers released him instantly, embarrassed at having spoken so plainly to him, and completely humiliated that she had allowed herself to touch him so personally.

"I'm sure Mr. Dupree wouldn't have brought her here if she's still dangerous, Rivers," Paxton assured her, taking her hand between his own and tenderly patting it. Then, looking to where Ruby stood talking with Jolee, he said, "I really should go make amends with Ruby. I was downright rude the other day in town." Then, affectionately pinching Rivers on the cheek, he left her.

Rivers watched him walk away from her. She watched him offer a hand to Ruby in greeting. Once again she began to doubt that Paxton had not truly loved Ruby. How could he not? The woman was beautiful.

"If my friend has kissed ya before like he kissed ya just now, you can quit your worryin', Rivers," Weston chuckled, coming to stand beside her.

"He's just a tease, Weston. You know it as well as I do," Rivers reminded him, blushing crimson all the same.

"Not when it comes to women, Rivers," he corrected her. "And lookee here at me. I've nearly gotten up my nerve," he added hesitantly.

"For what?" Rivers asked, somewhat preoccupied in watching Paxton and Ruby.

"For what? Are you joshin' me, girl? To ask Jolee to marry me!" he blurted out.

Rivers turned to him then, throwing her arms around his neck in a friendly and joyful embrace. Only such blissful news could've torn her away from watching Paxton's greeting to Ruby. "That's so wonderful, Weston! When? When will you ask her?"

"Well, this is certainly fickle of you, missy," the woman said.

Rivers released Weston and turned to see Mrs. Dupree standing just behind her, having watched them embrace. "Is Paxton aware of your unfaithful nature?" the woman asked.

"We're friends, Weston and I," Rivers explained.

"I don't doubt it," the woman said, turning from them and walking determinedly toward Paxton.

"She makes my skin crawl," Weston mumbled.

Rivers was curiously reminded of the evil witch-spider that had bitten Jolee. Marianna Dupree had the same essence about her the spider had—dark, threatening, harmful. Rivers could compare them and find the color of their bodies the only difference. She shook her head, trying to dispel the unnerving feelings, and turned back to her friend, forcing a smile once more. "Ask her soon, Weston. Soon. Then I'll . . ."

"Then you'll stay and be her bridesmaid, Rivers," Weston finished. "I know what you're thinkin', Rivers. But you can't leave—you can't leave Paxton."

"What do you mean?" she asked, turning from him.

"And there's no reason to. You belong here. You belong with that boy," Weston whispered, putting a comforting arm around her shoulders.

"Paxton doesn't want me any more than he wants pneumonia," she debated, even though his behavior toward her since the storm threatened to give her hope. "As soon as I see Jolee become your wife . . . I'll leave. I've got grandparents I need to be helping in their late years."

"He won't let ya leave anyway," Weston informed her as he walked away. Looking back over his shoulder at her briefly, he added, "You just try it. You little fly-sewer . . . you ain't goin' nowhere." He chuckled as he walked away.

Could it be? Rivers actually considered the

thought for a moment. Could it be Weston was right? Did Paxton actually value her—could he actually care for her?

Rivers watched as Paxton linked Ruby's arm with his and began walking toward the new barn skeleton. Immediately, what little hope had managed to sprout in her heart withered and died. Jolee caught sight of Rivers then and waved frantically, motioning for her to join them.

As Rivers approached Jolee, who had since been joined by Weston, she paused momentarily as Marianna appeared once more.

"Jolee, dear!" the woman exclaimed, seeming very overwrought. "Now, do tell me . . . you were bitten? By a spider? Is that it, dear?" the woman asked, seeming overly concerned.

"Yes, Mrs. Dupree," Jolee responded, taking hold of Weston's arm as if Marianna's presence frightened her. "A black widow."

"Oh, I've always admired the black widow spider," Mrs. Dupree sighed. "They're so . . . well, they know what they want, don't they? And such power over their mates . . . they kill their males, don't they?"

Each and every hair growing from Rivers's head prickled as she listened to the woman describe her admiration for the wicked arachnid.

"I think that makes them all the more frightenin' and distasteful, Mrs. Dupree," Jolee said.

"Oh, no, darling," Marianna cooed, smiling

wickedly. "That makes them all the more admirable."

Jolee's eyes widened, and she looked to Rivers, who was quickly becoming ill in the strange woman's company.

"If you'll excuse us, Mrs. Dupree," Weston said, tipping his hat to her. "I'd like to have Miss Gray to myself for a moment."

"Not at all, sweetheart," the woman cooed. She reached up and placed a dainty hand against Weston's cheek. "You run along, now. I believe Jolee's little friend can provide me with enough company."

Rivers's flesh began to crawl as Marianna turned her full attention to her.

"Well," she began, the look of revulsion apparent on her face once more, "Is Paxton merely an adequate lover or is he . . ."

"I . . . I wouldn't have the experience necessary to form an opinion, Mrs. Dupree," Rivers sputtered. The woman was obviously entirely insane, and Rivers looked about for some sort of polite escape.

Mrs. Dupree reached out, catching Rivers's chin in one hand. Rivers was shocked at her bold gesture and could only stare at her, stunned.

"You're lyin', you little tramp," the woman growled. "If I were to kiss him just now, I'd no doubt still taste you there!"

Rivers was so overwhelmingly shocked at

what the woman was saying she couldn't make to escape. She could only stare, horrified at such insanity roaming about free and virtually undetected. It wasn't until she felt Paxton's strong hand at her waist as he pushed Marianna's hand from her chin that she could even catch her breath again.

"She's such a lovely girl, Paxton," Marianna cooed. Her entire countenance had altered again. She was once more the elegant, pleasant lady she outwardly appeared to be. "You're a lucky boy."

"She's a friend of the family, Mrs. Dupree," he reputed. "Just a friend of the family, nothin' more." Paxton let his hand drop from where it had rested at Rivers's waist, but Rivers snatched his hand, holding it tightly for reassurance.

"Marianna, Paxton dear. Such formality is not necessary between us. We have, after all, been nearly intimately acquainted, haven't we?" Marianna said with a pungent air of implication as she turned and gracefully walked away.

"I've never met a woman who spoke so indecently," Rivers whispered.

"She'll be gone soon enough. Mr. Dupree told me the family is merely on their way to Hunnerton and is just stoppin' for a moment to pay their respects," Paxton explained. "If ya don't mind now, Rivers . . . my fingers are turnin' purple from you squeezin' them so hard."

Rivers immediately released her vice-grip on Paxton's hand.

"I'm sorry. I'm sorry. She just upset me." The terrifying visions bouncing about in her head needed to be spoken, and without waiting another moment she blurted, "She thinks you've some attachment to me, Paxton. She doesn't like it. You should've heard her talkin' about spiders killin' their mates! She means you harm. I believe that's why the family is back. She means to hurt . . ."

"She's just an insane woman, Rivers," Paxton reminded. "She won't hurt me."

"She stabbed her own husband, Paxton! She thinks that way! She thinks like that awful spider!" Rivers pleaded.

"You gotta get over that spider, girl. Spiders are spiders, and they serve their own purpose on this green earth." He smiled, seeming completely at ease. "Now, I gotta get back to this barn. You go find yerself a nice cool glass of lemonade. You'll feel better."

Rivers stood watching him walk away. She shook her head. Was he truly as blind as he pretended to be? Moments later, she was relieved to see the Dupree family climb into their wagon and drive away. Marianna had frightened her. For so long she had feared Paxton's memory of Ruby. Now, she wondered if her fears were misdirected.

CHAPTER NINE

Jolee shut the kitchen door behind her and leaned back against it, sighing heavily. "Oh, Rivers," she breathed. "He is so wonderful."

Rivers smiled, sincerely happy for her friend. "He's asked you, then?" she inquired.

"Asked me what?" Jolee puzzled. "Oh, no. Of course not, silly goose. He's only just kissed me good night out under that big, dreamy moon."

Rivers giggled. "Well, when you come down from flyin' around it, you just let me know."

Jolee sighed again and sat down at the table across from Rivers. "Wasn't that Mrs. Dupree simply frightenin'?" she asked. "She made my skin crawl. Just somethin' about her."

"She's mad. Completely mad," Rivers agreed. "Did you hear her goin' on and on about spiders? That is not natural."

"And the way she was pinin' after Paxton. I swear I saw her wipe the slobber from the corner of her mouth twice while she was starin' at him!" Jolee embellished, lowering her voice.

"Jo!" Rivers scolded.

Jolee giggled. "I'm sorry, Rivers. But I'm just too happy to think on such dismal things as that ghastly woman."

Rivers smiled once more. Jolee was truly in

love and completely blissful. She wouldn't ruin Jolee's joyous moment by continuing to talk about her fears.

"He'll ask you soon, Jo. I know he will," Rivers sighed.

"And then you can marry my brother, and we'll all live happily ever after," Jolee offered.

Rivers forced a smile and asked, "You'll marry Weston no matter what happens, won't you, Jo? You won't let anything stand in the way of it, will you?"

Jolee looked suspiciously at Rivers for a moment. Then, drawing in a knowing breath, she stated, "You're in love with my brother, Rivers, and you're afraid of him at the same time."

"What?"

"You're in love with Paxton. But ya can't bring yourself to believe he loves you. Or maybe you've got some strange idea he'll leave ya standin' at the altar like he did Ruby."

"Jolee, really now . . ."

"He won't. It's different with you. It'll all work out. You'll see, Rivers. You just have to let him go at his own pace," Jolee begged. "He's scared of it too."

Rivers shook her head. "No, no, no, Jo. You're in love and happy, and I understand that you want everyone around you to join in it with you. But you're the one who has to see . . ."

"Well, good evenin' there, girls," Paxton greeted, letting the kitchen door slam behind him as he entered the room. "Which one of you capable women is gonna trim my hair 'fore I take my bath tonight?"

"Rivers," Jolee volunteered, standing quickly and going to the cupboard. "I'll fill your tub for ya. I don't think Rivers is in any mood to find her backside soakin' in the tub again."

"All right then," Paxton agreed, yawning. "Grab them scissors, girl, and cut these curls off. I'm lookin' less and less like a man every day." Paxton reached over his shoulders, taking hold of the back of his shirt and swiftly pulling it off over his head.

"Here ya go, Rivers," Jolee said, handing Rivers a pair of scissors. "I've got to run to the outhouse for a minute." She winked at Rivers and dashed out the door Paxton had only just entered from.

Paxton yawned once more, this time stretching his powerful arms out at his sides for a moment before lacing his fingers together at the back of his neck. Rivers tried to avoid surveying his perfectly sculpted chest, shoulders, and arms, but her eyes took their own interest to heart and glanced quickly, yet thoroughly, at the man's well-developed torso.

"That old biddy ruffled your bloomers today, didn't she, girl?" Paxton asked.

"She's not right in the head, Paxton. And you know it," Rivers snapped, stepping behind him and pushing on one of his arms until he let them fall to his sides. As she lifted a lock of his hair, intending to snip the end, she marveled at the feel of it between her fingers.

"She is. I don't hold no argument with ya there," he agreed. "But she's not dangerous. You nearly squeezed my fingers clean off 'til she left."

"I'm sorry," Rivers sighed, snipping the end of the lock of hair and letting the trimming fall to the floor. "She just . . . she just . . . made me so uncomfortable."

Paxton chuckled. "More uncomfortable than that tornado bustin' up the barn above us the other day?"

Rivers submerged her hand into the thick sable locks at her fingertips, letting her fingers travel slowly through Paxton's soft hair and reveling in the way it clung attentively about her fingers.

Paxton closed his eyes, his teeth clenched tightly together, as Rivers's hand toyed with his hair. The girl's touch was like lightning striking him squarely in the top of the head. If she only knew the effect her mere touch had on his heart and senses, she'd run for cover for certain. If she only knew how much self-control he had, she would have to admire him.

146

• • •

Pulling his hair through her fingers, she quickly snipped the ends. And then, an impulse she could not ignore overtook her. Taking hold of one sable-soft lock, she snipped it entirely too close to his head, quickly reaching inside her shirtwaist and placing the lock of Paxton's hair inside her corset.

"Oops," she exclaimed.

"Oops?" Paxton inquired suspiciously. "Don't hack it up too bad, girl."

"It's fine," she lied. Quickly, for his nearness to her was all too exhilarating, Rivers finished clipping the hair at the back of his head and moved to stand before him. Immediately, she found it nearly impossible to reach his hair, for his long, muscular legs stretched out in front of him.

"You're gonna fall flat on your face or cut me bald doin' it that way, girl," he chuckled as he took her waist firmly between his hands. Pulling her toward him, he positioned her between his knees planting his feet on either side of her own so she could more aptly reach him.

Entirely unsettled by his extreme closeness, Rivers watched her own hands as they began to tremble and was nearly unable to steady them enough to continue trimming. At last, she snipped the last strands of hair and dusted them from her fingers. Then, she dared to look down into his magnificently handsome face as he tipped his head to meet her gaze.

Rivers felt her heart begin to hammer wildly, her breath quickening as she stared at him, unable to look away. Paxton's hands left her waist, one of the powerful appendages reaching up and clutching the collar of her blouse. Pulling Rivers down and forward, Paxton's mouth seized hers. Rivers was aware of the scissors slipping from her hand and falling to the floor as Paxton stood, gathering her into his dominant embrace, his mouth never leaving hers for an instant.

The dream-borne occasions in the past when Paxton had showered Rivers with his ravenous, capable kisses had been unimaginably blissful. Rivers had never in her life, prior to experiencing Paxton's kiss, even imagined a man could have such an effect on her emotions, body—her very spirit. She knew there could be nothing in the world more desirable, more wonderful, and more completely exhilarating than his kiss. Until, that is, that particular moment. Paxton had taken hold of Rivers's shirtwaist, pulling her into his embrace impatiently, all the while involving her in a kiss so hungry with uninhibited passion she feared her heart might burst and her mind might fail completely in its ability to remain sane.

The lock of his hair she had hidden inside her corset seemed to burn her flesh, making itself known as being part of him. Paxton's mouth left hers and traveled to her neck, allowing her to gasp and fill her lungs with life-giving air. He'd literally taken the breath from her with his kiss, and she still found the breathing process a difficult one as his lips and mouth toyed with the sensitive flesh of her neck.

Taking his face in her hands, she gasped, "Paxton, please." Directing his face forcefully, she pulled it from her neck so he stood gazing into her eyes. "You . . . you don't have to do this. Weston told me today he intends to ask Jolee to marry him very soon," she whispered. Letting her thumb caress the precious dimple at the corner of his mouth revealed as he grinned ever so slightly, she added, "You can quit tryin' to convince her that . . ."

Rivers was interrupted by the startling and somewhat shrill breaking of glass as an enormous rock hurled at them from outside the kitchen window. It landed on the floor at her feet.

"What in tarnation?" Paxton mumbled as he released Rivers, instantly striding to the door, angrily throwing it open and staring out into the darkness.

Still weakened from his kiss, Rivers clutched the back of the nearest chair and watched as Paxton peered out. "Jo?" he called. "Jo?"

At that moment, Jolee appeared in the doorway. "What on earth?" she asked, entering the kitchen and staring at the large rock and shattered glass strewn on the floor. "I heard someone runnin' off, Paxton . . . but I couldn't see . . ."

"Stay here," Paxton ordered. Without looking back to them, he stepped out of the house and into the dark.

"What happened, Rivers?" Jolee asked, retrieving the broom from its place behind the kitchen door.

"We were . . . I was cuttin' Paxton's hair . . . and that rock just came crashin' through the window," Rivers stammered. Her skin began to prickle at the knowledge being fed to her mind by her sixth sense. "It was Mrs. Dupree, Jo. You sense it too, don't you?"

"Oh, come on, Rivers," Jolee argued, though Rivers did not for a moment miss the involuntary shiver wracking her friend's body.

"She's obsessed with your brother, Jo. You know it as well as I do."

Jo bent down, pushing the rock out of her way and sweeping the glass into a pile. "You're obsessed with my brother, and you don't go throwin' rocks through folks' windows," she teased.

"What do you mean by that?" Rivers snapped.

"Oh, Rivers," Jolee giggled. "I'm only teasin'. But you have to admit, I'm a very kind sister. Why do you think I left you in here to cut his hair? I know how bad Paxton likes to corner you by himself. Shoot, I feel the same way about Weston. Our time alone together is very precious."

Rivers's heart began to break. She felt as if it were literally bleeding to death somehow. She had to confess—Jolee had to know the truth.

"Jo . . . he only pretends to . . . to be interested in me because he's been afraid you wouldn't marry Weston if . . . if you thought he would be alone. He . . . he wanted you to think he . . . he and I . . . he wanted you not to worry about him," she explained.

"What?" Jo asked, shaking her head in disbelief. "You're teasin' me, right?"

"No," Rivers admitted. "He asked me to stay until you were married because he was afraid you'd feel guilty about leavin' him alone and not marry. He's only been . . . he's only been pretendin' all the time." The confession hurt, caused Rivers's very soul to ache. With speaking the words aloud to Jolee, she'd realized how thoroughly she'd been fooling herself where Paxton was concerned. It was all a scene, an act in some horrible play. Even their moments alone—no doubt he'd just figured on enjoying himself while waiting for Jolee and Weston to marry.

"Rivers, Paxton would never use ya like that," Jolee scolded.

"Yes. I would," Paxton affirmed as he reentered the kitchen.

Jolee looked from her brother to Rivers and back. Then, reaching out and taking Rivers firmly by the shoulders, she said, "He's lyin', Rivers. I don't know why, but he is," she pleaded.

"Well, at least you know the truth. And you will marry Weston, won't you?" Rivers asked, forcing her lips to curve into a pleading smile.

Jolee looked to Paxton angrily and answered, "If for no other reason than to spite my brother, yes!" Then to Rivers she said, "He's lyin', Rivers. He'd never let ya leave him. There's somethin' he's not tellin'."

Rivers sighed, smiling and feigning relief.

"Well, at least the truth is out. No more play-acting. I'm tired. You don't mind if I leave you with this mess, Jo?" Without waiting for an answer, she left the brother and sister standing in the kitchen together, went to her room, and bolted the door firmly behind her.

Going to her wardrobe, she reached deep into its belly, retrieving the pair of boy's pants and the shirt she'd worn when first she'd arrived at the Gray farm. Mechanically, she removed her dress and petticoats and slid her legs into the trousers. As she watched her own fingers fumbling with the buttons of the shirt, her attention was captured by the lock of Paxton's hair tucked inside the top of her corset. She removed it, drawing it to her lips and kissing it gently before replacing it near her heart.

"You all right, Rivers?" came Jolee's concerned voice from the other side of the door.

"Just tired, Jo. Good night," Rivers answered.

"Well . . . good night then." Jolee sounded unconvinced.

Rivers sat on the edge of her bed, letting miserable tears of heartbreak flood her cheeks as she listened to Jolee's and Paxton's voices talking. They spoke for some time, but when she at last heard each one retreat to their rooms, the two doors closing behind them, she brushed the tears from her cheeks.

For the blessed and brief time in the kitchen when Paxton held her and kissed her so thoroughly, Rivers had begun to believe perhaps he did need her, want her, and even love her to some degree. But now she admitted to herself he did not—the time had come to leave. The train would pass the farm just after midnight. She knew it would, for each night since she'd come to the farm, its mournful whistle had interrupted her dreams of Paxton, calling to her, urging her to run away with it.

And so, she waited until the deepest hour of the night, when darkness was at its loneliest and the moon would illuminate the way. Picking up her boots, Rivers quietly left her room, creeping through the kitchen and closing the door softly as she stepped into the night.

Her tears had yet to cease. As she pulled on

her boy's boots, she hatefully wiped at them, resenting their presence on her face. The night was cool and clear, and the stars winked in the blackened sky like a million silvery gemstones. Yet, ominously, a thick cloud cover was inching in from the north. Rivers saw a light flash within their depths and knew that a storm was nearing. She only hoped it would hold itself at bay until she was on the train and sheltered.

Her heart seemed to hurt more intensely with each step she took away from the farm and toward the tracks. Her body began to ache for Paxton's embrace, not unlike a fatally wounded animal would ache for release from its existence. She thought of his mischievous smile, of the feel of his hair between her fingers. She smiled, remembering the look on his face after returning home one day having found the fly of his flannels sewn shut. She trembled at the remembrance of his lips on hers, the hot temperature of his kiss the day the rain had surprised them on their outing.

She stumbled then, catching herself just before her head would have hit a large rock. As she sat on her knees for a moment, her attention was drawn to the rock by a shiny thread twinkling in the moonlight. Bending forward to investigate, she was immediately seized upon by a sense of panic as she saw the large, shiny black body of the spider sitting amidst the sticky, silk threads of its web. The witch was quickly moving toward a moth entangled in her trap, and Rivers's mind was suddenly plagued with visions of Mrs. Dupree. Standing quickly, she turned and looked back toward the house. All was still dark within. She wondered if the frightening, unbalanced woman would try to hurt Paxton somehow. Sighing heavily, she turned and trudged forward, finding a pathway around the hideous spider and her pitiful, helpless victim.

Paxton's eyes strained to watch Rivers as she stumbled, paused, and then stood, moving onward toward the track. He tugged on his trousers, irritated and mumbling to himself, "You're a dang fool, Paxton Gray. What did you expect her to do?"

As he struggled with the button at his waist, he looked down for only an instant, but when he returned to look to the pasture once more, a fear like none he had ever known washed over him. The skin over every inch of his body began to crawl as he stood for a moment unable to believe the sight of the graceful being clothed in a flowing white gown following Rivers at a distance. In the next instant, without a care to his shirt or boots, he dashed from his room, shouting Jolee's name.

"Jo! Jo!" he hollered. "Get up, girl!" Jolee peered out her doorway.

"What in thunderation, Paxton?" she snapped.

"You run over and get Weston. Send him on over to the tracks to help me," Paxton shouted as he dashed toward the kitchen door.

"What's goin' on?" Jolee asked.

Before he disappeared into the night, Paxton paused for an instant—just long enough to growl, "Rivers has run off to the train, Jo. And I just seen Marianna Dupree followin' her."

CHAPTER TEN

Rivers uneasily waited by the tracks. She gazed with deep remorse at one large and brilliant star hanging in the heavens. Her father taught her to find direction by this magnificent beacon, but this night she felt lost and unable to sketch her way. She had never before worried about being caught hopping a train, but now something nagged at her. She was frightened, insecure, and terribly, terribly alone. As tears began to flow down her cheeks once more, she buried her face in her hands and let herself sob bitterly. She had never imagined there could be such heartache in mortal life, and she hated it with every breath of her soul.

"So, my little stone did scare you off."

Rivers jumped and quickly glanced up. She was horrified to see Mrs. Dupree standing before her. The woman wore an elegant white gown accentuating the ivory skin of her shoulders. Raising one daintily gloved hand to her mouth, she covered a small yawn before continuing. "I had meant to completely bean you with it, you understand. But I missed my mark, silly goose that I am," she sighed.

"Mrs. Dupree . . . you shouldn't be out like this. It's not safe," Rivers said.

"I followed you just to make sure he didn't, you understand. I was witness to your beguilin' manner of trickin' Paxton into kissin' you earlier this evenin'. And I'm not as yet convinced you haven't got my boy completely bound in your clutches. So—I thought I'd just come out here and wait with you."

Rivers was frightened. The woman was talking with her as casually as if they were at a church social sharing a glass of punch.

"It . . . it was only to make Jolee think he cared for me. He's afraid she won't marry if . . ."

Marianna Dupree lunged forward as she drew a knife from a pocket in her gown. Holding the blade at Rivers's throat, she growled, "Kneel, you little Jezebel! You kneel down!"

Rivers slowly dropped to her knees and watched in horror as the whites in Marianna Dupree's eyes burned red. "Do you really think he would even consider you when I've come back?" she asked. Slowly, Marianna Dupree again reached into her gown pocket and pulled out a larger knife with a jagged, serrated edge. Placing the tip of the knife to Rivers's bosom, she chuckled, "My husband uses these when he's hunting. They're very efficient weapons, you understand."

"Please, Mrs. Dupree . . ." Rivers pleaded in a whisper.

"Quiet, Jezebel. We'll just wait for the train . . . but don't upset me any further. If you do, I may

just have to quiet you somehow." She smiled—
the sweet smile of fleeting innocence of mind.

Paxton paused, commanding his angry body
to remain unseen. His first impulse was to rush
forward and pull Marianna away from Rivers.
He had to take time to think. Marianna held the
knife firmly against Rivers's throat. If he startled
Marianna, one little movement could fatally slice
Rivers's throat. He had to think! He couldn't risk
Rivers's being hurt.

"Marianna," Paxton said, stepping from the dark-
ness to stand directly behind her. Rivers felt
Marianna press the knife harder against her flesh.
She dared not draw more than shallow breaths.

"Paxton," Marianna whined in a disappointed
voice. "Paxton, you shouldn't have come. I
would've let her leave. But now you've come for
her and . . ."

"I've come for you, Marianna. Remember?"
Paxton corrected.

Rivers looked at the puzzled expression suddenly crossing Marianna's face.

"What?" she asked.

"We planned to meet. Remember, today we
talked about it and planned to meet here," he
said, his voice calm and soothing.

"I don't remember! Don't confuse me!" Marianna shouted. Rivers gasped as the knife at her

bosom moved down, tearing open her shirtwaist before Marianna stopped.

"I'm sorry, Marianna. I'm sorry. Don't be angry," Paxton said, kneeling beside the woman, but glaring at Rivers. Rivers met his gaze and knew her own eyes pleaded with his for deliverance.

"Don't look at him, you Jezebel!" Marianna screamed, slicing down and cutting Rivers's front corset lacings.

Rivers gasped and closed her eyes, afraid of what would happen should she dare to again look to Paxton for deliverance.

Paxton held his breath, and his inner voice silently shouted for help. Marianna was deranged—utterly mad! He dared not look at Rivers again for fear Marianna would make her threats a reality. He wished Marianna would turn her madness on him, enabling his precious Rivers to escape. A vision of Rivers dressed in his flannels and asleep on the straw pile in the barn burned through his mind—the first vision he really had of her—the moment his suspicions had been confirmed. He winced at the pain the memory sent ripping through his heart.

"Look at this, Paxton!" Marianna suddenly exclaimed, hurtling his mind away from remembering and back to the present. "Look what she's stolen from you! Take it! Take it from her!"

• • •

Rivers opened her eyes as she felt something moving at her bosom. Marianna's hands were occupied with holding her weapons to Rivers's throat and heart. It was Paxton who drew the lock of hair from Rivers's corset, studying it closely as it lay in his hand.

"Ah, let her keep it, Marianna . . . as a memento of what she can never have," Paxton said, smiling. He chuckled as he returned the lock of hair to its hiding place in Rivers's corset. Even for the danger of the situation, even for her life being threatened, still Paxton's touch sent goose bumps rippling over her body.

"Let's go, Marianna. Let the girl catch the train," Paxton said.

Rivers blinked, causing tears to trickle down her face. He was saving her life, and she knew it, but the tone in his voice was so completely cruel, so mocking.

Marianna wasn't convinced. She wickedly glared at Rivers. "I don't know, Paxton. You refused me once before. I'm suspicious that perhaps you really do care for this little Jezebel, and you're only tryin' to . . . tryin' to confuse me."

"Naw. Look at her, Marianna!" Paxton said with feigned disgust. "Dressed up like a man. How could she ever compare to you . . . you're womanly perfection," he flattered.

161

Rivers gasped as she felt the blade of the knife at her chest cut her flesh just below the hollow of her throat. The wound was short in length but deep, and she could feel the blood from the wound beginning to trickle down into her corset, gruesomely staining the lace edging.

"Wait!" Paxton shouted. His voice was not as calm as it had been a moment before. "Don't waste your time, Marianna. Let's go—you and me. Let's just leave her here and go," he urged.

Marianna looked to Paxton. She pressed the larger knife against Rivers's bosom once more. The smaller weapon she still held firmly against the young woman's throat. "You care for her, Paxton. You're lyin' to me."

Without any further warning, Marianna drew the knife from Rivers's bosom. Flinging her arm wildly in Paxton's direction, she severely sliced him across his bare chest. He groaned and put a hand to the wound.

"Look at you, Paxton," Marianna growled. "You didn't even take time to pull on your boots before chasin' after her, did you?"

Rivers looked and found that, indeed, Paxton's feet were bare and unprotected. In fact, the only clothing he seemed to be wearing at all was his trousers.

Marianna still held the smaller knife against Rivers's throat. Rivers dared not move and could only gasp in horror as the woman again sliced at Paxton with the large knife, leaving a deep wound across his stomach. Paxton was angry, and Rivers knew his restraint was for her sake. By the benevolence of the bright moonlight she could see every visible muscle in his body was tense and barely bridled.

"Let her go, Marianna. You can't butcher me good while you've still got one hand on her!" he shouted.

Marianna shook her head and said calmly, "I can't decide which one of you to butcher, you understand—you for being unfaithful to me or this little tramp of yours for seducin' you at every turn."

Rivers was further assured of Marianna's complete deterioration of mind as she saw Marianna hold the knife she used to cut Paxton to her lips, kissing its edge, still moist with his blood.

"I'm reminded of that spider we were discussin' . . . when was that? Remember . . . what's your name again? Rivers? Yes, Rivers. The spider that kills her lover when she's tired of him. Do you remember our talkin' of it?" Marianna asked, as if involved in no more than a casual conversation.

"You're mad!" Rivers cried out, unable to stifle her fear and frustration any longer.

"Quiet, girl . . . unless you want me to open your throat here and now!" Marianna growled, pushing the knife tighter to Rivers's neck. Rivers felt blood begin to run from the wound.

"Cut *my* heart out then, Marianna!" Paxton shouted, suddenly rising to his feet. The anger on his face was nearly as disturbing to Rivers as the madness of the woman who held her prisoner. "Right here!" he shouted, pounding on his chest with one mighty fist. "I hate you! I've hated you since the very first time I laid eyes on you! You make my stomach churn just lookin' at you! I would never consider . . ."

Marianna was at him then! One long, shrill scream and she released her hold on Rivers, flying at Paxton in a crazed hatred. Paxton was startled, and though he moved aside to avoid her attack, Marianna managed to drive the small knife she had held at Rivers's throat deep into his shoulder at the base of his neck.

Paxton shouted in pain. Rivers flew at the woman, trying to grab her wildly flailing arms, for the knives were still in her hands.

"You devil!" Marianna shouted. Turning, she struck Rivers across the face with barbaric force. Rivers stumbled to the ground as Marianna again turned on Paxton. Paxton grabbed her by the wrists, squeezing until she dropped the knives.

Paxton pulled Marianna to him, holding her arms at her back so she could not free herself.

"Paxton," Rivers breathed as she watched the deranged woman struggling in his arms.

"She's mad. Completely insane," Paxton muttered.

"I'm not," Marianna sighed. Her countenance changed, and she ceased her struggling, lovingly looking up into Paxton's face. "I'm sorry, Paxton darlin'. I was . . . I was just so jealous. You understand."

Paxton looked down at the woman in utter disbelief. "How can you possibly . . ." he began, but paused as the woman began placing tender, lingering kisses on his shoulders and neck.

Rivers watched in abhorrence as Marianna smiled up at Paxton between the kisses she placed on his body.

Paxton was unnerved. A revulsion he had never experienced was coursing through his veins, and on impulse, he shoved her away. His skin crawled with the lingering sensation of her kiss, and he could only stare at her in disgusted awe.

The whistle of the approaching train caught Marianna's attention. Rivers flinched as a sudden bolt of lightning illuminated the sky, revealing the woman's smiling and calm pleasant-appearing face.

"There's your train," she said, smiling sweetly at Rivers. Rivers could only look to Paxton, who stood bleeding profusely, still completely stunned by Marianna's actions. The thunder accompanied the next whistle blow, and the ground began to rumble as the lantern light of the train cut through the night. The familiar whistle distracted Rivers this time. As she glanced at the approaching train, Marianna leaped forward, snatching the knives from their place in the moist grass.

"Paxton!" Rivers screamed too late as Marianna turned, heaving one knife through the air and laughing hysterically as it embedded itself deep in Paxton's shoulder. Paxton crumpled to the ground, his body wracked with pain. Rivers stumbled toward him.

"No, dear. You've got a train to catch," Marianna giggled, attacking Rivers and holding the knife firmly against Rivers's abdomen. "Come along, Jezebel. Let's meet that train."

Rivers hesitated, and Marianna pressed the knife harder against her body. Grabbing Rivers's hair in hand, Marianna pulled hard, forcing Rivers back toward the tracks. Marianna giggled as she pushed Rivers onto the tracks, steadily increasing the pressure of the knife against Rivers.

"I don't suppose you've ever hopped a train in a predicament like this, have you, dear?" Marianna sneered.

Rivers looked to where Paxton lay in the grass, struggling to get to his feet. Suddenly, the blast of the whistle alerted her that the train was nearly on them. The engineer was no doubt in a state of panic at seeing two people on the tracks before him. He would know he could not stop in time to avoid crushing them. The whistle blew again, and Rivers started to move. Marianna slashed Rivers's trousers, cutting her deeply across the abdomen.

Rivers cried out in agony as Marianna shouted above the roar of the approaching engine, "Let the train take you, Jezebel. It'll be quicker. You understand."

Rivers looked to Paxton. Time seemed to slow as she saw him struggle to his feet. He bolted toward them. Taking Marianna's hair in one hand and the knife in the other, he threw her to the tracks. He shoved Rivers hard enough that she rolled free. Paxton stumbled and fell to his knees on the tracks as the train continued to rumble toward them. Rivers screamed! It seemed he could not possibly save himself. Miraculously, and only an instant before the powerful loco-motive ground Marianna's madness into the steel, Paxton threw himself backward from the tracks, narrowly avoiding the same fate.

Rivers collapsed to her knees, sobbing hys-terically as the train passed. The noise of the screeching on the tracks as the engineer tried to stop the monstrosity was deafening.

"Rivers," Paxton moaned, falling into the moist grass beside her.

"Paxton!" she cried, watching with horror as he pulled Marianna's knife from his body. "Oh, Paxton!"

Lying on his back and gasping for breath, he mumbled, "I'm sorry, Rivers. I've been such a fool."

A light rain began to fall as Rivers laid her head against his shoulder, which appeared to be the only part of his upper body void of severe laceration.

"You came for me. I can't believe you came for me," she whispered. She felt his hands on her head as he stroked her hair. Pulling herself up to sit beside him, her heart swelled with guilt at the knowledge she was responsible for his body being so painfully desecrated.

His hands lay on his chest. He closed his eyes for a moment as the rain fell on his face.

"I killed her," he muttered. "I killed her."

"No, Paxton," Rivers soothed, smoothing his hair back from his forehead as the rain fell there. "I saw her. She could've moved, just as you did. She chose not to. She stood up and met her fate full in the face."

It was true. As Rivers's mind horribly reviewed once more the vision she beheld just before the train crushed Marianna, she remembered the mad woman standing and stretching her arms at her sides, laughing maniacally.

Paxton shook his head from side to side and was silent for a moment before opening his eyes to glare at Rivers.

"You tried to leave me!" Paxton accused,

pulling himself to a sitting position, in spite of such dreadful pain. "I thought sure ya knew I was only . . . that I just can't say things . . . that I was . . . afraid to love ya completely, Rivers."

"You all right?" the engineer shouted as he approached. "She was laughin' when she went under. I ain't never seen anything like that!"

"We're fine," Paxton grunted, trying to stand. Rivers stood and took his hand, helping him up.

"Fine?" the man gasped as he studied the wounds on Paxton's body and the state of odd and immodest dress in which Rivers found herself. "Point me to the nearest farmhouse where I can get some help, mister."

"Yonder," Paxton said, pointing in the direction of his own farm.

"Thank ya. You all just stay right here. I'll go for help," the engineer assured them. He turned in the direction Paxton had indicated. He paused, however, adding, "Looks like folks is already comin' 'round."

Rivers looked and saw Weston and Jolee in the distance riding a bareback horse—Weston attired only in trousers and Jolee in her nightdress, hair blowing in the cool night breeze. The engineer sauntered off toward them.

Still weak, Paxton crumpled to his knees.

"Paxton!" Rivers cried. "Oh, Paxton, we have to get you home! You're so badly hurt." Once again the cool of the rain mingled with the salted tears on Rivers's face as she dropped to her knees before the man she loved. "She butchered you because of me."

"I would've let her cut my heart out to save you, Rivers," Paxton said, taking her in his arms. His pain-stricken body leaned against her own weakened one. Still, he bound her powerfully in his arms.

As the rain washed over them, rinsing the blood from their bodies, Rivers took Paxton's face between her hands and gazed into its beauty. Her thumb pressed at the corner of his mouth, forcing him to grin, revealing the beloved dimple there.

"I love you," she whispered. It frightened her to say the words aloud. Fear still whispered he would reject her confession. His response was not a verbal confirmation he felt the same. Rather, he placed a hand at the back of her head, drawing her nearer to him and blessing her with a deeply intimate and impassioned kiss, thoroughly enhanced by the refreshing rain streaming down their faces.

Rivers tasted the subtle salt of a tear as it touched her lip, finding its way into her mouth as Paxton drew away, gazing with adoration into her face. She realized then it was his tear she had tasted and not her own, for another single tear followed over Paxton's cheek to linger briefly on the curve of his lip before falling from his face.

"I love you," he breathed at last. "I love you so

hard it scrapes at my bones, Rivers. I'm sorry I couldn't tell you . . . show you . . . I'll never make that mistake again. I'll never hurt you again," he whispered. He grinned, pressing the lock of his hair more firmly into her corset. Then he grimaced as his eyes lingered on the wound at her chest. "I'm sorry," he mumbled, pressing a tender kiss to the hollow of her throat above the wound. Struggling to his feet once more, he groaned, "Help me get home, Rivers. I've got to get rested up so . . ." He paused, suddenly seeming puzzled. "I never told you I love you, Rivers . . . but didn't I show you enough sometimes? Couldn't ya tell by the way . . . the way ya sent me out of my head in the cellar? Or in the kitchen, for that matter?"

Rivers looked away, wiping a tear from her cheek. "I'm a wanderer, Paxton—plain and unexciting. Even at this moment, after you've said it to me . . . it's hard for me to believe it's true . . . that a man like you could truly . . ." she stammered, shy and still somehow fearful.

Paxton understood then. Finally, he understood why this beautiful young woman he valued and loved more than life could not believe he loved her. His mind reviewed quickly a conversation he'd had with his mother before she'd died.

"You're unusually handsome, son," his mother had said to him one day. *"I hope you won't use that gift to take advantage of women when the*

time comes. There will be some girls that'll think they deserve a man who looks like you do. There'll be some with wicked ways about them, and they'll want ya just because of the way ya look. But it's the one who doesn't . . . the one who's humble, sweet, pure, sincere, and sees herself as not good enough for you as a whole person . . . that's the one ya want, darlin'." He had never understood until that very moment what she had meant.

As a young man, Paxton Gray had all manner of women, of good report and bad, pursuing him. Not one of them had captured him until Ruby came along. He had admitted to himself, finally, that he'd committed to Ruby out of a sense of duty, but also as an escape. He had grown tired of the flirtatious ways of most women. The batting eyes and winks he found himself battered with at every turn. So, when Ruby had come along, ever insistent they were made for each other, he'd relented. But his conscience and will to direct his own destiny had brought him to his senses in time.

Now, standing before him—dressed in boy's clothes, tears streaming down her face, body bruised and bloodied because of him—was the very vision of what his mother had described that day so long ago. Paxton realized the "gift" his mother had spoken of was now his curse to bear. Rivers saw herself as a lesser, undeserving human being. Yet all the while she was the beauty—the gem that perhaps he was unworthy to hope for.

Dropping to his knees in the moist grass, Paxton held Rivers's waist in his hands as he looked up at her.

"I'm just a man, Rivers," he said. "Tall or short, handsome as a horse or ugly as a mud fence . . . I'm the same inside." He gazed up at her and continued, "I won't hurt you, Rivers. I love you the way a man loves only one woman—only one woman . . . forever. Marry me, Rivers, so I can prove it to you."

"I love you, Paxton," Rivers whispered, slipping through the embrace of his hands at her waist to kneel before him. "You'll never understand how much."

Holding her against him, Paxton brought her mouth to meet his in a moist, heated, impassioned kiss. His life-giving, reassuring, and magnificent kiss manifested thoroughly to Rivers his professed love for her was faithful and true. It was exhilarating to be in his arms! More so each time she found herself there. His mouth was hot and honeyed, and as she gave herself and her heart completely over to him, she was acutely aware of how happy she was at his confessing his unfeigned love for her.

"I like this better when you're in your drawers," he whispered. She forced a scowl at him in reprimand. He chuckled and before resuming his previous endeavors teased, "Let's see . . . there's got to be an old root cellar around here someplace."

EPILOGUE

Rivers awoke late in the morning, the morbid and tragic visions of Marianna and her death foremost in her mind's eye. Now . . . now that it was over, now that Paxton was out of danger, she could pity the poor madwoman. Something had fouled Marianna's mind and caused her unwanted lunacy. Rivers wondered, though, if she would ever be able to dispel the horrid visions of that night from her memory. The sounds were still ringing in her ears now and again—the sounds of Paxton's body being wounded, the sound of the train screeching to a halt. However, the visions would be the worst to endure. Yet she knew time would somewhat fade them at least, and it gave her hope of eventual peace of mind.

As she dressed, her thoughts turned to Paxton, and rejuvenating warmth spread through her. Paxton's wounds were much more profound than hers. He had been nearly irrational when they returned home and he had seen in the brighter light of the lantern the damage done to her. He had insisted her wounds be tended before his own. While Jolee cleaned and bandaged her injuries, Paxton paced, incessantly asking about her state of health. She basked in the thought he cared so deeply for her.

"Well, I don't know about you, Rivers," Jolee

began as Rivers entered the kitchen, "but I want my own weddin'! I don't care if you and Paxton have yours first . . . but I want my own. Do ya think I'm terrible?" Jolee's happiness in her anticipated marriage to her beloved Weston perfumed the very air and lightened the heavy burden of the memories of the night for Rivers.

"What are you talkin' about, Jo?" Rivers asked. She hadn't mentioned the conversation she and Paxton had in the dew-covered grass near the railroad tracks.

"Paxton told me this mornin', when he first woke up. He said ya never answered him exactly but that he was purty sure you'd agreed to marryin' him. I knew he was lyin' last night. And now I know why. He's got that same sixth sense you do, Rivers. He knew Marianna was millin' around, and he figured out why."

Rivers nodded, but her thoughts still lingered on one fact—that after all that had happened, his being butchered, Marianna's horrible fate— Paxton still managed to tell his sister he'd spoken of marriage to her.

"I'm goin' out for a jar of peaches," Jolee stated, standing up and moving toward the door. "I'm gonna make a pie for Weston's supper."

"No, no, no," Rivers said smiling. "Let me go. The fresh air will do me good."

"You will not!" Jolee argued. "You sit back down there and . . ."

176

"Oh, Jo," Rivers sighed as she pushed past her and through the door. "I'm fine." She didn't mind going to the cellar for the peaches, even if she was sore and aching. As soon as she retrieved the peaches for Jo, she would search out her heart's desire. She would spend the day with Paxton, for she knew he was too injured for hard work.

As she walked out toward the cellar, she thought how wonderful life would be. Weston and Jolee living close, their children and the ones she and Paxton would have playing together on the front steps. Paxton's children! The thought forced a sigh of excited satisfaction from her lungs and into the fresh morning air. Was she dreaming? She still wondered if she were.

As Rivers stood in the cellar looking around for a nice jar of peaches, doubt began to fill her mind. Surely Paxton couldn't really be hers. He was too wonderful! Too handsome! Too desirable!

Rivers gasped, and her thoughts were interrupted as the cellar door suddenly slammed shut. She was unsettled as she stood in complete darkness. Yet when she heard Paxton's roguish chuckle, she turned, instantly relieved and delighted by the sight of him.

"I feel a storm brewin' in here," Paxton said as he lit the lantern, the tiny flame lighting the darkness.

Rivers looked up, gazing into his handsome face, mesmerized at the way his eyes seemed to flash in the dim light. Reaching out, she softly caressed his bandaged shoulder.

"What are you doin' out of bed?" she asked as he set the lantern down and gathered her into his arms and against the strength of his warm, powerful body. Rivers laid her palm against his whiskery cheek, pressing her thumb into the dimple at the corner of his smile.

"Jolee doesn't trust me where you're concerned. So . . . I figure 'til we're married proper, these private moments are gonna be mighty rare."

"*I* trust you," Rivers said, lost in the deep blue of his eyes.

"Oh, I know ya do. And dang it all . . . if that won't force me to keep in line," he said. "Maybe."

His mouth captured hers then in a ravaging, savory kiss—a powerful, loving exchange—evidence and promise of the eternal felicity they would know together.

Author's Note

I wonder sometimes if most people simply skip the dedication in the front of a book. I never do—I always read the dedications from the author. I find them interesting and very curious, especially considering that most of the time, they're rather vague or seem to hold some mystery about them. I love that! Furthermore, I think the dedication of a book is important merely because it often reveals something about the author and his or her life and inspiration. Don't you think so? Therefore, as my little (and perhaps trivial) author's note for *Sudden Storms* begins, let us take a look at the *Sudden Storms* dedication, shall we? In case you missed it, here it is again:

To Sheri
For all the glorious adventures we've
shared . . .
Photo fun and betta fish sprees,
Belting out ballads in yogurt parlors . . .
And the Sudden Storms of life we've
weathered together.
Thank you for being the blessed and
bright sunshine after the rain . . .
For rare and true friendship to cherish—

*and memories like no others in
the universe!
Thus, for you . . . some kisses in the rain!*

Sheri—my cherished friend of over 15 years. Sheri—my partner in silliness. Sheri—who makes me laugh like no one else can. Ahhhh, Sheri—easily my most hilarious friend! The adventures that Sheri and I have shared over the years are truly too numerous to mention. Just for fun, here's a short list (and I do mean short) that, in the interest of time, is void of the best and most hysterical details:

1. As the girls from the 80s pop music group the Groovy Chicks, I fronted as the actual lead singer, and Sheri was not only a member of the backup (and the only one who could still actually fit into her authentic, vintage 80s clothes) but also served as the silent MC for an event, dressed in nothing but a pair of men's long underwear and an orange tutu ballerina costume whilst whirling about to the "Fractured Fairy Tales" theme music.
2. Sheri taught me the magic of rubber cement where working with photos and art projects is concerned—long, long, long before scrapbooking was the concept it is now.
3. Together Sheri and I took our children out into the bay in Birch Bay, Washington, waded

up to our bosoms in the water, and collected approximately 300 expired (meaning dead) sand dollars. Painstakingly, we soaked and cleaned them in bleach, dried them in the sun, divvied them up, and then wondered what in the world we were going to do with them.

4. Any kind of photographic devise (like a camera or photo booth) is always made more adventurous with Sheri in the mix. Props are also her forte. Give her one of those paper toilet seat covers, a cutout of Legolas in Barnes & Noble, or a giant rocking chair, and look out!

5. With Sheri, I've seen what happens when she yells, "Look at that!" while standing in a field of tulips surrounded by a busload of camera-toting tourists from Japan.

6. We have skipped through acres of blooming daffodils with our arms wide-spread while singing at the top of our lungs. And on that same adventure, we discovered that salmon jerky is disgusting, and therefore girls on girl trips should always bring their own snacks to eat while attending the Tulip Festival because otherwise salmon jerky is the only thing to be found at roadside stands!

7. With Sheri I have attended Neil Diamond concerts that, because of her company, were epic! At one such event, after we stood in our seats, arms raised and swaying while joining Neil in

a chorus of "Sweet Caroline," we walked back to our hotel in the Portland, Oregon, midnight rain as it drenched our matching Christmas sweaters and soaked us to the skin. Fabulous!

8. Traffic jams are never fun—unless one is traveling with Sheri, as my photograph of Sheri trying to hitchhike a ride from a passing ambulance during that famous traffic jam will prove. During that infamous hour-long traffic jam, Sheri and I gathered bouquets of wild sunflowers midst grass that grew higher than our waists. Ahhhh! Only Sheri can make such a frustrating situation one of the best memories of your life.

9. Then there was the time we went on a betta fish buying spree! Naturally we named them all. One betta in particular, who seemed to have a rather more active elimination system than most, we christened "Poopalotta." And Poopalotta lived up to his name for years and years until he finally passed on to that great betta bowl in the sky.

Together Sheri and I have taken photos in bed and breakfast bathtubs and photographed old houses, gates, seals, giant rocking chairs, carousels, restaurant food, and fellow passengers on airplane flights. We've done the Twelve Days of Christmas for years and years for one another. We've held shadow puppet performances on the bathroom floors of restaurants, cracking up fellow bathroom attendees. We've had luncheons in Victorian tearooms where we wrapped ourselves in fox and mink furs and took pictures. Long before digital photography, Sheri was using her amazing graphic design talents to "crop and paste" us into photos with Elvis, Sergei Grinkov, and Antonio Banderas.

All this fun and frivolity doesn't even begin to scratch the surface—nor does it even hint at all that Sheri has taught me, the tears and heartache we've helped each other bear, or the trials and tribulations we've weathered together. Sheri has been not only my friend but my teacher, guide, and personal healing clown for many, many years.

Thus, to a cherished friend who adores nature and plants and especially rain, I wrote this little novella, *Sudden Storms*. So you see, the dedications in a book do mean something to the author—or at least to this author they do.

Which leads me to my next topic of random rambling—kissing in the rain! What is it about kissing in the rain that intrigues not only my bosom friend Sheri but seemingly all romantic hearts, huh? I mean, think about it—movies are packed with kissing in the rain. Let's just take a moment and list a few movies: *The Quiet Man* (a very famous kissing-in-the-rain scene, and one of my favorites), *Spiderman* (of course),

The Notebook (Hello? Totally famous!), and *Australia*—to name only a few that come to my mind. Kissing in the rain seems to be a favorite lyric thread for songs too.

So why is everyone (including Sheri) intrigued with rain kissing? Well, my theory is this: rain is refreshing, liberating, and dreamy somehow. Have you ever been caught in an unexpected rainstorm? It sort of throws your emotions and physical senses for a loop. At first, you might be like, "Oh no! I'm going to get soaked!" But then, once you realized you're going to get soaked and there's nothing you can do about it, you're kind of like, "Oh well. There's nothing I can do, so why not just jump in a puddle or play with some tadpoles?" Do you know what I mean? I think that "oh well" moment is the moment of liberation— the moment where we realize (at least for girls) that our hair is going to be ruined, our mascara is going to run, and, if we're wearing a white shirt, everyone is going to know what color of bra we're wearing, so what the heck—we might as well jump in a puddle or kiss a guy we've always wanted to! Do you know what I mean? There's just something liberating about being caught in the rain; something is let loose inside us—care, worry, previous plans.

In truth, rain is a therapeutic thing in so many ways. Think about it—how delicious is it to sit in the house curled up on the sofa, all cuddled in a soft fleece blanket, listening to the rain outside while eating chocolate and reading a good book? It's wonderful! Now admittedly, having lived in Washington state, too much rain can be somewhat depressing—at least to me. But I'm talking about summer thunderstorms kind of rain—maybe some far-off echoing thunder mingled with huge, refreshing raindrops. It just frees the soul somehow, tears away inhibition.

Furthermore, there's something about the idea of being wet when kissing, right? It's like—I don't know—wildly exhilarating or something. So combine exhilaration, refreshment, inhibition, liberation, and the human tendency toward romance, and there you have it! That's why we all love the idea of kissing in the rain. That's why we all love to kiss in the rain. Of course, that's my short "kissing-in-the-rain-for-novices" version. Hmmm. I think I could maybe write a nonfiction book on that subject.

Anyway—onward. Lane. Yep. While sitting there beginning to write *Sudden Storms* all those years ago, I glanced over at my cedar chest (most likely piled with clothes needing to be folded or something) and saw the name Lane. Yep. A Lane cedar chest—that's what I have.

"What does this have to do with the price of tuna?" you might be thinking. Well, nothing—but Lane is the name I "plugged in" to *Sudden Storms* at that moment, the original name for the hero. Yes, Paxton Gray was originally Lane Martin. *Totally* not a name I would normally stick with. But this was back in the day (as I've explained before) when I used to plug in any old name and then forget to go back and change it later. So there you have it—Paxton Gray once went by the alias Lane Martin. Crazy, huh?

Just as crazy is that Rivers's name was originally Tamara! I know, huh? So not me! (Though I like the name and know some great Tamaras.) Jolee Gray was originally Joella Martin, her boyfriend Weston having gone simply by Steve. Sometimes I get a real kick out of my past self because I wanted to change the names right when I'd finished the book. But a then-friend of mine literally threw a tantrum and was so upset that I was going to change the names that I knuckled to peer pressure and didn't. What a wiener I was back then. And where does that saying come from anyway? When someone is weak and spineless, we call them a wiener. Hmmm. Interesting.

And yet onward still. Now, correct me if I'm wrong, but I do believe that this was the first book I wrote that included the subconscious revelation of one of my greatest phobias: arachnophobia, to be precise. Yes, it's true. Before poor Cassidy had her morbid spider experience in *Shackles of Honor*, Rivers and Jolee had theirs in *Sudden Storms*. Spiders completely wig me out! They don't wig me out as much as they used to because I've worked on being braver—more courageous and self-reliant when it comes to dealing with them. But they still wig me out! For the first thirteen years or so of our married life, it was quite common for Kevin to come home from work and find a quart Mason jar or two (or perhaps a Ball jar, depending on which brand was close at hand during my time of need) sitting upside down in the middle of the kitchen or living room floor. Why? Because I couldn't squash a spider! They freaked me out so badly that it took every ounce of bravery I could muster just to reach down (usually from my perch on my knees on a kitchen chair) and put a Mason jar over one. I just couldn't squash them, and I certainly didn't want them running off to prowl around my house, so I'd just gather every thread of guts I could, and I'd put a Mason jar (or a Ball jar) over them and let Kevin kill them when he got home. Ahhhh! Yuck! Yickee! Goose bumps (the bad kind)! And fear and trembling! I hate spiders! And I especially hated them years ago. (To be intentionally redundant, I've worked on handling my arachnophobia over the years so that I'm pretty good at squashing them now—if they aren't too big, that is.)

So, in case you hadn't picked up on it already, I hate spiders. I used to have nightmares about them quite often—especially black widows! Which is kind of odd when you think about it, because black widows kind of run in my family. Not the murdering-human-ladies-who-want-money kind you see on made-for-TV movies—just the real kind, the spider kind.

One of my first memories as a child is a little vision of my mom standing on our front porch with a glass quart jar in hand (could've been a Mason jar—could've been a Ball) catching black widows and popping them into the jar. I'm serious! She'd catch as many as she could in one jar and just set the jar out on the front porch. After a day or two, you'd go out there and there'd only be one black widow left alive in the jar— one big, plump, shiny, red-hourglass-abdomined champion. Ewww! Mom always said she didn't want them hanging around the porch because they were dangerous, and she didn't want to be mean and squish them. What? So she left them in the jar and let them duke it out to the death? Oh yeah, that's humane! She's so funny sometimes.

My mom was always intrigued with black widow spiders. I think it stemmed from the fact that she is so very scientifically minded—interested in everything. Couple that with the fact she had a teacher in high school who would pick a black widow spider up by the body with his thumb and forefinger to allow his students a closer look at her legs, spinners, hourglass, and other features, and you have black widow spider intrigue at its finest. (As a side note, that crazy teacher never was bitten—at least not in my mom's experience—and she was always amazed at his bravery.)

While thinking about all this spider stuff, I called my mom today and asked her why she was so intrigued with black widows and why in the world she used to catch them in quart jars.

"I was always intrigued with them, and I think I just caught them for the fun of it, I guess," she answered matter-of-factly.

"For the fun of it?" I exclaimed.

She laughed and said, "Well, yeah."

Knowing my mom as I do—knowing her adventurous character and insatiable curiosity about all things in nature—I said, "And you probably liked the risk."

She laughed again and said, "Yeah. Probably for the risk too."

She also told me this little story about when she was growing up—and I quote: "One of their (black widows') favorite places was the old outdoor toilets . . . down under the seat in the hole. We kids were always afraid to go out there, especially Sharon (her younger sister) and I, and my mom would say, 'Oh, just go out there and wet on 'em! They're not gonna bother you.' But sometimes we'd sneak out behind a weed or something anyway . . . or out in the barn or behind a tree or something." Ah! Life in the sticks—you gotta love it! And miss it too.

As for me, I remember our "laundry room" at home. It was actually outside the house in a separate building out in back. Every summer, there were black widows lurking all over in there. (Consequently, I hated doing laundry.) Well, one day, my mom came in from doing laundry. She was reaching over her shoulder to her back and was sort of loosely fisting some fabric at the back of her shirt.

"Come here, Skeeter," she said all calm and rational-like. (Skeeter is my nickname, of course.)

"Yeah?" I innocently asked as I approached.

"I think a spider dropped down the back of my shirt while I was in the laundry room," she casually explained.

"What?" I probably screamed.

"I think it's a black widow. I saw one on the ceiling out there when I went in," she added.

"What?" I screeched. "Mom!"

Well, sure enough—once my mom and I had managed to unbutton the front of her shirt and remove it from the arm that wasn't clutching the fabric at her back, she let go of the fabric, and there she was—a big ol' black widow spider! Ahhhhhhhhhhhhh! (I'm all itchy right now just remembering it!)

Black widows are aggressive, you know. They're not as easy to scare off as other spiders. I remember my dad trying to stomp on one out in the garage one day. Did it run away at the sound of his stomping, at the sight of his big, old boot coming at it? I say unto thee, nay! It ran right at him, up onto the toe of his boot, and started up the rest of his boot toward his leg before he finally reached down and squashed it!

Right now you're thinking, "Well, surely that's the end of the black widow spiders in the family stories." But no! Among the many, many, many black widow stories in my family—several of them having to do with jars, in fact—is the one my Uncle Wayne tells about my Aunt Sharon (my mom's little sister who was afraid of the black widows in the outhouse, remember?). Well, apparently my auntie (my Aunt Sharon and my mom and Uncle Wayne's sister) had spent an undetermined amount of time collecting black widows in a jar of her own, one day way back when. Hmm. Let me begin again.

So (curious again to get the story right from the horse's mouth as it were) I paused a moment in my pointless spider rambling here and called my auntie.

"Auntie? What's that story about you and the black widow spiders in the jar again?" I asked.

"Oh," she began as casually as if she were preparing to share a recipe. "I just went out all day long one day and collected black widow spiders and put them in a jar, punched holes in the lid, balanced the jar lid (no ring) on the jar, and slid it under my bed. During the night they must've all bunched up at the top and pushed the lid off because when I woke up in the morning, the lid was off and all the spiders were gone."

I know—the women in my family are crazy! Keep in mind Auntie said she was probably about ten years old when she did this. My Uncle Wayne tells the story because he is a fellow arachnophobic—which is actually kind of ironic being that he's the one who recently taught me how to kill rattlesnakes and skin them. He always tells the story of Auntie's escaped spiders like it's the worst horror movie a guy could ever watch. He's three years younger than Auntie and was old enough to know that an entire Mason jar (or more likely a Ball jar, being that it was back in the early fifties) full of black widow spiders was loose in the house.

Auntie's final casual remark on the matter was this: "Hmm . . . that's probably why the house was crawling with black widows for a while that year."

So you see, black widows run in my family— as does arachnophobia. Just a little trivial insight into the inspiration for Jolee's black widow experience in *Sudden Storms*.

I would feel as if I'd really failed—miserably failed—if I didn't mention to you the good ol' *Sudden Storms* Party of 1996. Yep—I'd just finished writing *Sudden Storms* and was getting ready to have surgery to remove a huge ovarian cyst, so naturally I decided to have a party! Oh, the preparations I made were quite detailed. And it was so much fun.

First of all, the handwritten invitations were embossed (I was into embossing then). The night of the party (the night before I ended up in the hospital a day early for my surgery), each guest was handed an envelope as they arrived. In each envelope, there was a *Sudden Storms* bookmark, a raffle ticket, a bunch of play money, and some other stuff I can't remember right now. As the evening launched, each guest could go to the "general store" and buy things such as a shred of Jackson McCall's shirt, a toothpick that Michael McCall had chewed on, or a rock that Paxton Gray had put in his pocket to use for skipping on the pond later. One could also purchase things to eat, like bacon or homemade bread. Guests could also have their photo taken with "Paxton Gray," who arrived in the middle of the party with a cowboy hat full of Hershey's Kisses that he handed out to all the ladies. Yep! This young man, who was my friend's son and a friend of our family, dressed up like the *Sudden Storms* hero, arrived to a soundtrack of a thunderstorm, and said, "There's a sudden storm a-brewin'!" as he entered the house. All the guests then spent their time standing in line to pay their twenty dollars of toy money to have their picture taken with the hero. He'd even swoop you up in his arms if you'd let him. It was hysterical—totally fun! There are many more details that I can't remember right now. But I do remember how fun it was. I wish we could do that same thing now. But I guess we kind of do, don't we? Each summer at the Meet and Greets? How fun! (P.S. No black widows were involved at the party. Thank heaven!)

Are you simply astonished at how long I can blabber on and on about trivial things? But that's just me, I guess. And I do hope you enjoyed getting to know a little bit more about my inspiration for *Sudden Storms*—or at least that I'm an arachnophobic with black widow collectors in the family. You just never know what's lurking in my brain or what might inspire me to write. Right?

Sudden Storms Trivia Snippets

Snippet #1—*Sudden Storms* was the first book wherein I tried to force a character out of the truth of himself. I actually forced Paxton (Lane at the time) to have "tawny-colored" hair. Consequently, I couldn't sleep for like seven years because of it. I hadn't been true to the character. Thus, Paxton now sports his true hair color in *Sudden Storms*—"sable-smooth" and "onyx-black."

Snippet #2—Yes, it's true. One of my dad's favorite practical jokes was/is sewing the fly shut on men's underwear. I did it a few times growing up—even as a grown-up. I sewed the fly shut on the underwear of one of Kevin's friends several years ago, and unfortunately, Kevin's friend wore that particular pair of underwear on a fishing trip—you know, when he was all garbed up with everything tucked in and wearing those rubber fishing pants and rubber boots. It proved, shall we say, a difficult time for him, and I've always felt bad. That was the one and only practical joke I've ever allowed myself to be involved in since.

Snippet #3—Like Paxton, my Grandpa States played the harmonica. I loved to hear him play and have always, always wished there were some tapes of him playing.

Snippet #4—The only "school club" I was ever in was the Rock Hound Club in elementary school. I *love* rocks! To this day, I love them—and, admittedly, I collect them here and there. I'm also fascinated with skipping rocks over the surface of large bodies of water. I really don't get the chance to skip rocks much—being that I live in the desert—but when I do have the opportunity, I could spend hours just skipping rocks and skipping rocks and skipping rocks.

Snippet #5—You know the scene where Paxton and Rivers and Jolee and Weston are out on the picnic and there are some drawings on a big rock formation nearby? Well, here in Albuquerque, we have the Petroglyph National Monument located on the Westside. The petroglyphs are rock carvings, most of which were made by Pueblo Indian ancestors between 1300 and the 1680s, with many that date much earlier. The petroglyphs depict animals, people, brands, and so forth and are very intriguing to study. So, once again, real life inspires!

Snippet #6—In the 1950s, Northrop Aircraft Incorporated used black widow spiderweb filaments as crosshairs in microscopes and telescopes for Army tank sights. Black widow webs were used for gun sights during World War II through the 1960s. In 1943, the US Army Quartermaster Corps set up an entire "web collection" operation to help with the production of gun sights. (This is information I originally learned as a child from—you've got it—my mom!)

Snippet #7—Among the many necessary life skills my mother passed on to me is the uncanny ability to easily and instantly recognize a black widow spiderweb. Oh, believe me, I can spot a widow web from a mile away! Black widow webs are different from other spiderwebs—no visible pattern to them, just a sort of chaotic appearance, even though they are carefully constructed. Though mom taught me to recognize them by touch too (they are shiny and super sticky, with quite a different feel, different than other spider webs), I don't have to touch one to identify it as that of a black widow. **Helpful Tip of the Day:** Happen upon a black widow in your garage? Most over-the-counter insecticides won't do her in. But spray her with a high-grade hairspray and you can disable her long enough to scream for Kevin to come finish her off!

About the Author

Marcia Lynn McClure's intoxicating succession of novels, novellas, and e-books—including *The Visions of Ransom Lake*, *A Crimson Frost*, *The Rogue Knight*, and most recently *The Pirate Ruse*—has established her as one of the most favored and engaging authors of true romance. Her unprecedented forte in weaving captivating stories of western, medieval, regency, and contemporary amour void of brusque intimacy has earned her the title "The Queen of Kissing."

Marcia, who was born in Albuquerque, New Mexico, has spent her life intrigued with people, history, love, and romance. A wife, mother, grandmother, family historian, poet, and author, Marcia Lynn McClure spins her tales of splendor for the sake of offering respite through the beauty, mirth, and delight of a worthwhile and wonderful story.

Center Point Large Print
600 Brooks Road / PO Box 1
Thorndike, ME 04986-0001 USA

(207) 568-3717

US & Canada:
1 800 929-9108
www.centerpointlargeprint.com